Defiant Heart

By Tracey Bateman

DEFIANT HEART

Coming Soon

DISTANT HEART

Defiant Heart

Tracey Bateman

AVON
INSPIRE
An Imprint of HarperCollins*Publishers*

HarperCollins books may be purchased for educational, business, or sales promotional use. For information please write: Special Markets Department, HarperCollins Publishers, 10 East 53rd Street, New York, NY 10022.

FIRST EDITION

Interior text designed by Elizabeth M. Glover

Library of Congress Cataloging-in-Publication Data

Bateman, Tracey Victoria.
Defiant heart / Tracey Bateman.—1st ed.
p. cm.
ISBN: 978-0-06-124633-3
ISBN-10: 0-06-124633-6
I. Title.

PS3602.A854D45 2007
813'.6—dc22 2007060705

07 08 09 10 11 ID/RRD 10 9 8 7 6 5 4 3 2 1

Dedicated to Mom

You bought each of the *Love Comes Softly* books as fast as Jeanette Oke and her publisher could get them on the shelves. Those books began my love for prairie romance when I was only ten years old and twenty-seven years later, I still love reading historical romance about the pioneers who dug out this country one shovelful at a time. And now I'm privileged to write them as well. Thank you for helping me frame my future. I love you.

DEFIANT HEART

One

1850

The folks of Hawkins, Kansas, had only two reasons to get excited on any given day. One: the birth of a baby (which only happened in the rooms above the saloons but, nonetheless, gave cause for a stir), and two: a wagon train making camp along the creek just outside of town for one, two, sometimes as many as three days if the Oregon-bound settlers were ahead of schedule and needed to make repairs to more than a couple of wagons.

Today there were no babies reported born, but the town was up in arms just the same, and that could mean only one thing: The first wagon train of the year was about to make camp just beyond the town's border.

"It's a'comin'!" The disembodied shout from outside the store window caught Fannie Caldwell's attention and brought an intake of air to her lungs. Every nerve ending beckoned her to run to the door and join the small gathering of townsfolk—men, mostly, except for the occasional fancy woman venturing sleepily from one saloon or another, face paint smeared, shawls drawn over petticoats and chemises.

As much as Fannie longed to venture out herself, she knew better. She could feel Tom's eyes boring into her. Those dark, leering eyes that followed her wherever she went. Hour after hour. Day after endless day. Year after year. She had to remain alive and whole if she was going to keep Kip and Katie alive and whole, so she stayed put, keeping her gaze focused on the account books open on the counter in front of her.

Grunting, Tom pulled his bloated body from the wobbly wooden chair at the end of the counter. Disgust burned a hole through Fannie as the middle-aged storekeeper lumbered across the scarred plank floor. He grabbed hold of the leather latch, yanked open the door, and stepped out into the dusty street.

"Gal," he called with gruff command, "you best git your head out of them books and ready the store for business. This one looks to be a long train—pert near a hunnerd wagons I'm guessin'."

Fannie's heart lifted at the news. A wagon train that big could surely hide three small people like her and the twins. Maybe things were finally starting to go right for a change. A grim smile tugged at Fannie's lips, but she squelched it before Tom could see. No sense raising his suspicions.

"Ya hear me? Or do I need to help yer hearin' a mite?"

They both knew he wouldn't beat her just now. There was no one else to run the store for the next few hours. Too much money to be made and not enough time for her to take a beating, then pull herself together for what promised to be a busy day of selling. "Yes, Tom. I heard you."

"Git to it, then."

With a sigh, Fannie did as she was told. She'd learned long ago the price of disobedience. Not that she was a lily-livered coward. But after three years of being indentured to Tom, she knew all too intimately the pain of connecting with his fists, boots, the flat of his hand. And tonight there was too much at stake for her to risk provoking a beating she might not be able to recover from very quickly.

"Yes, sir." The sound of her soft submission masked the wild rebellion nearly exploding from her heart. The subservient reply would have fooled even the most astute bystander. Thankfully, it fooled Tom. It had to. If her plan was going to work.

Fannie shut the account book and shoved it beneath the counter. Next, she set to work dusting shelves and raising prices 50 percent as Tom always insisted. Enough so that he made substantially more of a profit than his already overpriced goods demanded, but not so much that the average traveler, hungry for the sight of a town and the inside of a dry goods store, would balk too much before plunking down the price.

"Where's Kip?" Tom barked. The planks groaned beneath his mass as he reentered the store and waddled to his seat. "These folk'll need someone to help carry packages." Another two bits per customer. Another shot of whiskey for Tom.

Fannie forced herself to maintain an air of calm. "He'll be along soon. Remember, last night you told him to go to the creek this morning and catch fish for tonight's supper?"

"Huh? Thet right?"

No. It was a flat-out lie, but he'd never know it. The drunken fool. Kip and Katie weren't anywhere near the creek. They were loading the wagon with the last of the supplies they'd smuggled out last night after Tom drank himself unconscious. Lookouts had been reporting back on the wagon train's forward progress for the past two days. The three siblings had gone to work finalizing preparations at the first word. If all went according to plan, by the time Tom drank himself into the same inevitable stupor tonight, she and the twins would be long gone.

When the first wagon came into view through the open door, Fannie could no longer resist the pull to stare. The longing she kept carefully hidden. Tom had spoken the truth. All told, there must be a hundred wagons, maybe more. She knew they would pull through town and make camp just the other side, next to the creek.

Within the hour, the first wave of pioneers would find their way into the store. By nightfall, her body would ache with fatigue. Tom would hover for a while then, as the money box got fatter and fatter, his excitement would grow, and he'd leave her to the wagon train customers and visit one or both of the local saloons. Eventually, he'd stagger home rip-roaring drunk. She wouldn't think about what would happen later, but afterwards, when he fell into a stupor, her plan would fall into place. Three years of meticulous planning. She finally had everything she needed to take Katie and Kip away from this godforsaken dirt pile of a town. If a person could even call it that. Two saloons, a smithy, and Tom's trade store. That pretty much summed up the town's commerce.

Tom made a killing during the hot, windy days of summer on the Kansas plains, when the slow-moving wagon trains rattled through, ready to replenish their supplies or buy fripperies to make the pioneers feel normal again after weeks on the dusty trail. Unfortunately, Tom's seasonal mother lode never led him any closer to wealth or respectability. He wasted every penny during the winter keeping his gullet filled with whiskey.

That was just fine with Fannie. The longer he stayed away, the less likely he'd be in any shape to mess with her. Or Katie. Katie's plight worried her the most. So far Tom kept his distance from her twelve-year-old sister; but lately, Fannie had noticed his black eyes roving over strawberry blond hair, the budding figure, wide pale green eyes that astoundingly still shone with innocence. All these features were precursors of the beautiful young woman the little girl would soon become—only a fool couldn't see Katie's potential—and even Tom wasn't that much of a fool. Fannie clenched her fist against the sudden knot in her gut. The pig would never touch a hair on her sister's head. Not while she, Fannie, had breath in her body.

Fannie shifted as familiar anger twisted through her like a prairie storm. He'd never get within ten feet of Katie. That was part of the bargain. But then, when had Tom ever kept to a bargain?

Three years earlier, Fannie's body had trembled with grief, fear, outrage, betrayal as she watched the money exchange hands from the storekeeper to her stepfather, Silas, and knew there was no turning back. Nothing was going to save them. The sale was final.

Silas had refused to meet her eyes as he cleared his throat, pocketed the fifty dollars the fat, stinking storekeeper had just handed over, and slipped out the door of the dusty storeroom without a word of farewell. The no-good stepfather couldn't even wait until Ma and their baby brother were cold in the ground before breaking his promise to take care of the three of them.

Nine-year-old Katie had innocently whispered, "Where's Pa going, Fannie?"

"He's not our pa," Fannie said with great ferocity. Their pa had been a fine, decent man full of laughter, love, and stories of the Wild West. His death had been Fannie's blackest day. Until Silas met Tom.

Fannie had slipped her arm around the little girl's shoulders and jerked her own chin high, refusing the threatening tears burning her eyes. It was okay for the kids to cry. But not her. She was in charge now, and she had to stay strong if she was going to give the twins strength.

Tom's tongue slid over his sickening, thick lips as he eyed her up and down. Eyed Katie and gave Kip a quick dismissive glance. "Now, I don't want any trouble out of ya's," he grunted, moving his girth forward, first one massive leg, then the next until he stood directly in front of Fannie. "Thet clear?"

His stench nearly knocked her over as he towered above her, and she fought to keep from retching. When she didn't answer right away, he grabbed her chin with two meaty fingers and forced her to look into his lustful gaze. "I done asked ya a question."

"Yes, sir. It's perfectly clear that you prefer us to be obedient." She forced perfect grammar, perfect diction, and just a touch of arrogance as she spoke like her Eastern-born mother had always taught her.

His bushy, unkempt eyebrows pushed together in a frown, and his eyes clouded over with stupid confusion. A wave of superiority washed across Fannie's heart. This fool would never win a battle of wits with even the dumbest dog, let alone someone with an ounce of brains. If she could keep him from hitting them, she'd have no trouble fulfilling the two years she'd heard Tom agree to. Two years, he'd said. When she turned sixteen, she'd be fully grown and old enough to make her own decisions. Then she could leave and take care of the twins on her own.

But he had not kept his word and one year after her service should have ended, Fannie found herself and her brother and sister still trapped, slaves to a cruel pig of a man who had no intention of ever letting them go, short of his death . . . or theirs.

Fannie shook herself from the familiar resentment that accompanied her memories and the injustice of a broken word, the first group of pioneers descended upon the tiny store. The travelers were no different in demeanor than so many others Fannie had observed over the past three years. Weary, slumped bodies showed the wear of the endless work that accompanied life on the trail, but the eyes . . . oh that crystal spark of hope that shone brightly in the men and women who dreamed of a lush paradise. The land of milk and honey. The Promised Land.

Fannie smiled at each as they came to the counter to purchase the exorbitantly priced goods. No one seemed to mind. She studied each face. A line of freshly scrubbed children followed their parents.

"For a tablecloth and curtains once we get our cabin built," the woman explained with a hesitant upward curve of full lips that mirrored those of her children as she presented a length of blue gingham.

Fannie found herself relaxing in the presence of this smiling family. She hoped they would become good friends. And if she wasn't mistaken, a couple of the children were around Kip and Katie's age. That was good. Maybe they'd learn to smile too.

The door swung open, bringing with it a blast of hot, late-spring wind. Fannie caught her breath as a tall form filled the doorway. He wore buckskins and a pair of moccasins and had the lean but well-muscled appearance of a man accustomed to the hard, disciplined life on the trail—the life Fannie had only dreamed of. He stepped out of the blinding sunlight, and as his features came into view, Fannie's mouth went dry. Dark hair curled on the ends, and dark eyes scanned the room as he entered the store and took ownership of everyone's attention—even Toni, the town's most famous harlot, who Fannie could see was making a beeline for the man. He walked with an air of confidence that somehow made Fannie feel brave. No doubt about it. This fellow had to be the wagon master—just the man she was looking for.

Blake Tanner cast a glance around the scratch of a general store and pressed his lips into a grim line. Marked-up prices and second-rate goods. He knew this place well. And half a dozen just like it between here and the Platte River. He'd done his best to warn the folks not to pay the prices, but the travelers needed a diversion and ignored his advice. Well, let them learn the hard way. He'd done his best. The choice belonged to them. But this would be the last time he gave in very easily. If they didn't reach across the mountains before winter, they'd have to hole up somewhere. With this many people to feed, who knew if they had enough supplies to last the several months they'd be stuck. He couldn't bear the thought of losing even one hopeful pioneer who had signed on to his wagon train, trusting him to get them from Independence to Oregon in one piece.

If he'd had his druthers, the wagon train would never have stopped, but repairs needed to be made, and there was no smithy among them. Hawkins afforded them the one available blacksmith for at least another month—provided he could keep the train on schedule; otherwise, no telling how much longer it might be before another opportunity arose. And Blake knew from leading half a dozen trains over the Rockies that he'd lose at least fifteen wagons, maybe more, before rolling into the lush, Willamette Valley if the wagons weren't strengthened before the crossing. With repairs, they might only lose three or four.

Better to allow a one-day, two at the most, stopover now.

The store was filling up fast with members of his wagon

train. Blake fought the temptation to escape the suffocation he always felt in confined spaces. But the weight of responsibility hung on him like an anvil, and he wanted to keep an eye on things. Especially on Willard James. Blake couldn't quite put his finger on why . . . but he didn't trust the father of six. He'd figured out long ago if a man seemed too friendly, too generous, too hardworking, he was most likely too good to be true. And this Willard was the friendliest, most generous, and hardest-working fellow he'd ever met. One of those traits would have been enough to raise Blake's suspicions; all three traits made the man a downright criminal in Blake's mind. And he was taking no chances he had a thief in his train—someone who might just give the train a bad reputation. News traveled fast in these parts. One disgruntled, wronged rider who went ahead and started whispering discontent could induce a posse to meet his wagon train on the outskirts of the next town. Or the next. And sometimes—like now—the future safety and success of the wagon train depended upon being allowed to enter a town and buy supplies.

Willard and his shy, unassuming family moved past in a single line, smiling, arms filled with goods, and filed out the door. Blake was just about to hightail it out of the store where he could breathe, when a soft hand touched his arm, gently commanding his attention, compelling him to turn. Sweet perfume wafted to his nostrils even before he caught full sight of the source of the scent. A dirty shawl draped around pink shoulders, the threadbare article poorly concealing a rounded bosom that left little to the imagination. Smeared face paint and dark shadows under her eyes bespoke morning-after fatigue. His stomach churned as memories of his own mother flooded him. Recoiling from the woman's touch, he jerked his arm away.

Her brow puckered at his reaction, but Blake made no apologies.

"Please," the voice was deceptively soft, feeding Blake's repulsion. "Mr. Tanner?"

"That's right."

"You're the wagon master?"

"Right again."

Her gaze flicked nervously toward the door. "I want to join your wagon train."

Blake grunted a short laugh and gave her his back. "No."

She grabbed his arm, igniting his anger, and yanked at him until he faced her once more. "Don't turn away from me, sir. I've seen the advertisements for brides out West. I-I want to be one of them."

"Those ads aren't meant for women like you." She disgusted him. "Leave me alone, lady."

Her face turned scarlet but she squared her shoulders. "My name is Toni, and, as you've already pointed out, I'm no lady."

"A man's name?" He gave a snort.

"Short for Antonia, not that it's any of your business."

So, the woman had spunk. A haughty woman of her profession would be easier to say no to than a woman given to tears and tantrums.

"Doesn't make any difference. My decision stands."

To his chagrin, the woman continued to press. He hated brazen women. "N-none of the advertisements say what *kind* of women they're looking for." She pulled a torn, newsprint article from between her breasts and shoved it toward him. "See? There it says *wives* sought."

"I'm not taking a woman like you to meet up with some unsuspecting farmer looking for a decent *lady* to share his life and land with. It wouldn't be right."

Desperation clung to her, crumpling the bravado she'd displayed only seconds before. Her eyes sparked with pleading. "Please. I'm through with this life. I just need a chance to get away from here. I-I can pay."

He glanced over her, fighting to keep his disdain in check. "I don't need your kind of money."

A loud smack of flesh on wood arrested his attention. "What's wrong with you, mister? Don't you have a heart?" Blake swung around to find the source of the indignant words. The accusation shot across the room from the counter. The first thing he noticed were enormous blue eyes and a mass of unruly red curls springing from a poorly executed chignon. At first glance, she looked like a child in need of braids rather than a grown woman with pinned-up hair.

The girl traveled the room in no time flat and stood unflinching before him, her face hard as granite, eyes cold as sapphires. She appeared no taller than a ten-year-old boy, but with one sweeping gaze over a well-rounded figure, Blake knew she was past childhood. He swallowed hard and averted his gaze back to the beautiful eyes.

"Well?" She glowered at him. "Why can't Toni go with

you? If no man wants to marry her, she can go back to work. Don't they have brothels out West? She'd probably make a killing."

Toni placed a calming hand on the other woman's arm. "It's all right, Fannie."

"No it isn't all right. Who is he to say you aren't fit to join his wagon train? He doesn't even know you."

Blake studied the one called Fannie. She was either incredibly kind or incredibly dumb. Still, he had his duty. "No women like her. No unaccompanied women period. No widows with children—unless one of them children is an able-bodied boy of at least fourteen years old. No women who don't have a man to look after them."

The young woman's eyes grew even wider. "Wh-what do you mean, no women traveling without a man?"

"I think I've made myself perfectly clear." A stubborn smile lined his face. "I make the rules, and my rules stand."

"But why? I—I mean she can work hard too—just as hard as any man, I bet."

He gave a carefully thoughtful nod, and bit back a grin. So she was one of those women who wanted to compete with men. Who thought they should have the right to vote and own their own land. "Hard workers are always needed."

Triumph lit her beautiful eyes, and her full mouth curved into a smile that nearly knocked him off his feet. "Well, then . . . ?"

He gathered himself and steeled his heart. "There's still one problem."

"What's that?"

"I don't allow unaccompanied women on my train." He turned his attention back to the floozy. "Find yourself a husband first, and maybe I'll make room for you. Otherwise . . ." He let the silent words speak for themselves.

The girl named Fannie stomped the dirt floor. "But that don't make any kind of sense whatsoever! And only someone touched in the head would suggest such a thing."

Beautiful or no, this young woman was beginning to grate on his nerves like a squeaky wheel. Why wouldn't she just take no for an answer?

"Is that so?"

She nodded and jerked her thumb toward the other woman. "She wants to go west to *find* herself a man. Didn't you hear her? She's not interested in any of the riffraff around these parts. She's looking for a good man to marry up with. Not some drunk mountain man who only wants to relive his biggest bear kill."

Toni sniffed as her eyes filled with tears, but she composed herself just as quickly. The quick action drew Blake's admiration in spite of himself. She leaned in closer to Blake, and whispered. "If I don't get away from this town, I'll die. I'll just die."

"Hiram!" A woman's high-pitched scold sliced through Blake's foolishness. He glanced beyond the prostitute to the husband and wife headed their way. The man was trying hard not to stare at Toni, but he wasn't doing a very good job of hiding his lust. His wife's mouth pursed in indignation, and her eyes sparked anger as she swept her skirt aside lest it touch the prostitute. Blake pressed his lips together in steady resolve. He didn't envy that man once his wife got him alone and started in on him. Not that he blamed her. Still, this was the sort of contention he couldn't encourage by allowing immoral women along.

Blake slipped his fingers through his thick hair. As much as he'd like to help this woman, this scene would be the inevitable if he were to allow this fancy woman to join them.

Blake turned back to Toni, but she refused to meet his gaze.

"And that is exactly why you're not coming with us." So saying, he slapped his hat on his head, took one more look at Fannie, whose face was mottled with anger. She jerked her chin as she deliberately looked away and placed an arm around the distraught Toni's shoulders.

Two

Fury exploded in Fannie as she stared after the bullheaded wagon master. "Don't mind him. We'll figure out a way." Fierce determination gripped her shoulders, drawing them straight and proud. "Even if we have to go it alone."

Toni shrugged her off and turned sharply, her eyes narrowing to catlike slits. "What do you mean 'we'?"

Fear licked Fannie's insides as she realized her mistake. She glanced about to be sure no one had overheard. If Tom got wind of her plans, he'd kill her for sure. Besides, the last thing she needed was to be saddled with a fancy woman who probably couldn't even hitch a pair of oxen to a wagon—not that she was much accomplished in the task herself. "Never mind. I meant you. You'll find a way to make him change his mind. I best get back to my other customers."

"Anyway," Toni breathed, defeat quivering in her voice. "I best get back before George finds out I was talking to the wagon master. Not that it did me any good."

Compassion tugged at Fannie's heart. She squeezed the

young prostitute's hand. "Don't give up. The wagon train doesn't pull out 'til morning."

Toni peered closer, her luminous amber eyes searching Fannie's face until Fannie was forced to turn away. "You were going to ask Mr. Tanner if you could join the wagon train too." As though she knew the danger for Fannie should word get out, Toni kept her voice to the barest of whispers. "Weren't you?"

Fannie knew there was no point in denying the truth. She nodded. "I have to get my sister out of here, or Tom . . ."

A barely perceptible nod inched Toni's chin up, then back. "I understand. What will you do? You hear what Mr. Tanner said. I don't think it's going to be very easy to change his mind. Women aren't allowed in his train without a man."

A fresh surge of anger tormented Fannie, bringing with it helpless frustration. "I'd rather be strapped to a hungry bear."

Toni grinned. "Me too."

A sense of camaraderie hung in the air between them, and Fannie warmed to the notion of having a companion on the trail. But only for a moment. She had her brother and sister to think of. She couldn't worry about anyone else.

If only the wagon master would stop being so unreasonable. Who did he think he was anyway? She should have told him just what she thought of a bully throwing his weight around. Just because she wasn't a man didn't mean she couldn't do the work of a man. Did he honestly think she was going to cause trouble? Or was it just Toni's profession? The man had been downright hostile to the prostitute. The thought raised Fannie's hope. Perhaps if she met with him alone, she could reason with him. Show him she wasn't the same type of woman as Toni.

An uncomfortable image of Tom forking over fifty dollars for her invaded her mind. But she shoved it aside. No. She wasn't the same. She couldn't be. Her ma hadn't raised her to be that type of woman. She would never give in willingly to any man.

"Excuse me," a haughty voice called, arresting Fannie's attention, pulling her from thoughts of what she should have said to that varmint. "I'm ready to pay for my purchases." The sour-faced woman who had swept aside her skirts at the sight of Toni now stood at the counter, tapping her foot with rapid impatience while her roving-eyed husband tried not to stare at Toni's bare shoulders.

Pressing her hand to Fannie's arm, Toni leaned in close, and whispered, "I'll be back later to find out if you've thought of a plan."

Before Fannie could respond, the fancy woman hurried away. Fannie's face twisted into a scowl. She certainly didn't need to be saddled with someone else to take care of. She had nothing against the prostitute. She had enough troubles of her own, to think about the rights and wrongs of other people's lives. Besides, Toni had always seemed like a good sort. But that didn't mean Fannie wanted the attention brought on by traveling with a harlot.

How was she going to get out of this mess?

But there was no time to think about it for now. The line at the counter had grown beyond the husband and wife and extended all the way to the door.

For the next several hours, Fannie kept busy with the constant influx of wagon train customers. Most were friendly, some were not, and she made a note to beware of the more impatient and downright sour among them. One thing she'd learned over the past three years was that self-preservation demanded she pay attention to moods, attitudes, and body language. With Tom that could mean the difference between being left alone and being beaten black-and-blue. She preferred caution. It proved much less costly.

Even now, she stayed on her guard. Every time the door opened, her heart picked up with a beat of fear. No telling when Tom would be back, drunk, spoiling for a fight and anything else he wanted from her.

Kip and Katie were still at the old abandoned barn three miles outside of town, where they had stored all the goods and the wagon for the trip. Hank Moore, the town smithy, had boarded the oxen for them during the past three months. Fannie didn't know why the kindly blacksmith was helping her out. So far, he'd asked for nothing. But Fannie wasn't counting on his good nature and kind heart. She was waiting for him to call in his favor.

By the time the sun sank low on the western horizon, the last of the customers were just leaving the store. Fannie exhaled in relief and arched her back in an effort to find relief from the ache. With a sigh, she pulled the account book from the shelf. Today had been the most profitable day they'd ever had. At least since she'd been doing the accounts. It wasn't difficult to fool Tom. He was arrogant enough to believe she was too afraid of him to make even the simplest mistake, let alone put in false numbers so that she could take what she figured was her fair share anyway.

Deftly, she counted every penny in the cash box, took a few bills off the top, and tucked them into her waistband, then went to work balancing the figures in the books against the new cash.

The door flew open, giving her a start. She pressed her palm to her chest as Kip and Katie breezed in. Both were out of breath and swallowed hard to get a word out. Kip's deep auburn hair mirrored their mother's, and sometimes Fannie longed to reach out and touch it. But Kip was too old for that now and didn't like to be coddled. So she let him be. Katie's hair showed more blond than red and bordered on what Pa had proudly called "strawberry blond." Kip had recently begun to exhibit signs that he was growing into a man, just as Katie exhibited signs of womanhood. His shoulders were a bit broader, and his voice moved up and down at times, bringing quick blushes and angry fire in his eyes should anyone dare draw the slightest attention to the fluctuations. Fannie respected his privacy, as did Katie. Tom was another story and delighted in humiliating the boy whenever possible. They would be coming to blows soon—another reason for Fannie to get the twins away from the brute.

"What are you two up to?" Fannie demanded. They couldn't take any chances of angering Tom tonight. Another whipping like Kip had gotten last month, and they'd miss the wagon train for sure.

"They're having a dance."

"Who?" Fannie carefully locked the cash box and placed

the key in the secret hole under the counter where Tom would undoubtedly look when he got home and count his profits for the day.

"The folks from the wagon train. They got their wagons in a circle, and they're dancing with a fiddler and everything."

"Can we go?" Katie asked, her wide green eyes pleading.

Fannie's heart pinched, but she knew she couldn't give in.

She leaned in close to the pair and kept her voice deliberately soft. "There'll be plenty of dances along the way. We can't take a chance on getting Tom all riled up. Understand?"

"Aw." Kip kicked at the dirt floor with his scuffed boots.

Taking the boy by his shoulders, she forced him to look her in the eye. "Do you understand that we have to be extra careful tonight?" He scowled.

Frustrated, Fannie turned to Katie. The girl nodded solemnly. "We understand, Fannie." She nudged her brother. "Don't we, Kip?"

A belligerent shrug lifted his broadening shoulders. "Yeah. We understand."

Thank heavens for Katie's positive influence on the lad. "All right. Is everything ready for us to go?"

Kip perked up, his eyes bright with hope. "All we got to do is hook up them lazy oxen. Mr. Moore done brought 'em to the barn. Still don't know why we couldn't just get us a couple of horses."

"Because horses aren't as practical over the long haul. Oxen won't wear out as fast. Do you understand?"

He gave an uncharacteristic nod of submission. "I guess that makes sense."

Relieved that one more argument had been averted, Fannie gave voice to the concern she'd been mulling over for the past few months. It was one thing to get away in the first place. Quite another to keep from being recaptured.

"Now we have to figure out how to get away from Tom and keep him from bringing us back when he finds out we're gone. The wagon train will move a lot slower than he could on horseback."

The one good thing about Hawkins was that the townsfolk had never gotten around to finding a sheriff. Only riffraff and the occasional farmer frequented the town. It was doubtful Tom would be able to find enough men to go after her. But the thought of losing his slaves might be enough incentive to cause him to hire folks to bring them back.

"Why don't we just shoot him?" Kip asked, his eyes fierce with hatred.

"And be wanted for murder?" Fannie scowled at the boy. Not that she hadn't had the same thought. But they couldn't act impulsively. "We can't trade one prison for another, Kip. We have to use our heads."

An idea was beginning to form in Fannie's mind as she glanced out at the darkening sky. "Tom's going to be home wanting his supper soon. Katie, go to the cold cellar and bring up the stew from last night and mix up a batch of biscuits to go with it."

"Here." She took the money from her waistband and passed it to Kip. "Put this with the rest. I have to go out for a little while. You stay here, and don't take your eye off Katie if Tom gets back before I do."

Fear lit the little girl's eyes. "Don't go, Fannie."

"I won't be gone long. He won't try anything with Kip looking after you."

They all knew she was lying. But there was no choice. Fannie had to try and reason with the wagon master.

She stepped out into the warm, windy night and glanced surreptitiously toward both of the saloons. Loud raucous laughter and poorly played music sounded from the buildings. Was the wagon master in either of the saloons? He'd been walking in that direction when he left the store earlier. She shook her head. She couldn't chance having Tom spot her. Instead she turned her steps toward the outskirts of town to the wagon train. Perhaps, with a little luck, she would be joining that train in the morning. But first she had to find a way to convince the wagon master to change his mind.

Blake stood outside the circle of wagons listening to the sounds of laughter and merriment, his foot tapping in unconscious rhythm to the fiddler's rendition of "Old Dan Tucker." He would have enjoyed a turn around the campsite with Mrs. Cooper, a pretty young widow traveling with her father-in-law and four-year-old son. She'd made no secret of her interest in him, and he saw no reason not to enjoy a dance or two with a willing partner. Instead, he was forced to look out for latecomers like a nervous mother waiting for her daughter to come home from her first Sunday afternoon buggy ride with a new beau.

Frustration bit hard inside of him. He'd given strict instructions that everyone must return to the wagon train by sunset. There were at least six men, including Willard, still unaccounted for.

"Maybe town wasn't such a good idea."

Sam Two Feathers stood beside him. The half-Sioux scout was Blake's best friend and the best tracker in the West. His sharp instincts had kept every wagon train Blake had taken West safe from more than one Indian or outlaw attack over the last five years.

Blake expelled a puff of air. "Too many folks needing repairs to avoid town this time."

"I suppose. Want me to go round up those men? They're probably drunk as skunks by now."

If anyone could, Two Feathers could do it, but even dressed in white men's style of buckskins identical to Blake's, there was no mistaking Sam's Sioux features. "No sense asking for trouble. Let's just keep an eye out for them so they don't disrupt the train when they came home. Note each man that stayed out past curfew and put him on for extra duty in the morning. And make sure they don't enter camp. They'll sleep outside the circle tonight on the hard ground. Maybe that'll make them think twice before disobeying orders next time."

Two Feathers nodded, then cocked his head. "Someone's coming. On foot."

"You're slipping." Blake fingered his six-shooter but grinned at his friend. "I saw her coming five minutes ago."

"As did I." Sam returned his smile. "I'll leave you to talk to the woman."

As the slight form entered the glow of the firelight, Blake drew a quick breath. The eyes were unmistakable. The last time he'd seen them, they were shooting daggers in his general direction. "Are you lost?"

She jerked her chin up. "No. I was looking for you, Mr. Tanner."

Blake hitched his leg up and rested his foot on the tongue of the nearest wagon. "You have me at a disadvantage, Miss . . ."

"Caldwell. Fannie Caldwell."

An interesting name for an interesting young woman.

"What can I do for you, Miss Caldwell?"

"I have a team of oxen, all the proper supplies, and a wagon ready to go. I have to be part of this train when you pull out in the morning."

"Why didn't your pa come and talk to me?"

"My pa's been dead since I was ten years old." Fannie's heart pinched as it always did when she remembered her real pa. The only gentle, kind man she'd ever known.

"So it's just you?"

"And Kip and Katie. My brother and sister."

"Well, have your brother come and see me before the wagon train pulls out in the morning, and we'll do what we can."

Squaring her narrow shoulders, the woman planted her legs in a defiant stance. "Kip's twelve years old. I do the talking for the family."

"I see. Well, I'm sorry, Miss Caldwell. But I do the talking for this wagon train, and you heard my policy regarding single women joining alone."

"Why are you so dad-blamed stubborn?"

Ah, there were the flashing eyes. Even in the dim glow of the fire, they shot through him like flaming arrows, piercing and burning a place in his heart he'd just as soon guard. "Stubbornness is an unfortunate trait I received from my mother."

Her lips curled into a sarcastic sneer. "I'm sure she's a charming woman."

Determined not to give an inch, Blake scowled right back. "She's dead, and when she was alive, she wasn't a bit charming except when she wanted to be. Like most women."

She jerked her chin with stubbornness that refused to feel compassion. "What about me joining the wagon train?"

Lord help him, he wanted to throw away his principles and allow Miss Caldwell a spot. But he knew better than to be fooled by a pair of amazing eyes, an attractive spray of freckles across her nose and cheeks, and an unruly mass of hair a man could plunge his fingers into. Attractive women were a dime a dozen. The cost of maintaining discipline on his train demanded a much higher price. He had to stick to the rules. No matter how much he might be tempted to toss them out for Fannie Caldwell's blue eyes or one grateful smile from her beautiful full lips, he knew better. It was one thing to allow an aging widow with a back of steel and hands of iron who wasn't afraid of hard work—like Sadie Barnes. But this woman was a different story altogether. She seemed sincere enough now, but in the light of day they were all the same. Conniving, manipulative, and willing to do or say anything to get their way. He steeled his heart and shook his head firmly. "Nope. No single women."

Quick tears glimmered in her eyes. Blake swallowed hard,

unbelievably affected. "Look, don't cry. I wish I could help you, but those are the rules, Miss Caldwell."

Anger, swift and hot glared back at him. "Who's crying? I don't cry, mister. And I don't beg. I'll get west with or without your help." She spun on her heel and stomped away, leaving Blake staring after her wishing like the dickens he could call her back and tell her he'd changed his mind.

"Pretty girl."

Blake jerked around, irritated that he'd allowed himself to be distracted enough not to notice that Two Feathers had come back.

"Thought you went to check on the men."

"Someone is following the girl. Thought I'd make sure she gets back to town safe."

"Following? What do you mean? I didn't hear anyone." Blake felt like a fool for being so absorbed in Fannie's exhilarating presence that he'd neglected to stay aware of his surroundings.

Two Feathers didn't gloat. Rather, he accepted the situation for what it was. Though Blake could count on one hand the times he'd been too distracted to sense danger—or the potential for such—he'd always been grateful for his friend. And now was no different. Sam kept his voice low. "I'll go after her."

Blake nodded. He couldn't leave the wagon train without leadership while they were camped outside of a rough town like Hawkins. Though everything in him fought to leave Two Feathers in charge and see to Fannie's safety, he knew where his responsibility lay. "Make sure nothing happens to her."

Sam didn't respond but faded silently into the night. As much as Blake wished he was the one going after the girl, he knew he didn't need to worry, with his Indian friend taking care of matters. Sam was the only man he trusted to take care of things as well as, if not better than, he could. And that was a high compliment.

He looked into the sky for just a moment and stared at the glittering stars, the soft glow of a half-moon. The kind of moon that made a man think maybe something existed beyond the earth. The notion of God was starting to grow on him. Thanks to Sam's confounded preaching night and day. And there was something about sleeping under the stars every night that made a man aware of the existence of something bigger than himself.

Although he hadn't been raised anywhere near a church and no self-respecting, God-fearing man or woman would have anything to do with the likes of him and his mother, Blake had always lived an honest life, tried to be just and fair in his dealings with folks. But Two Feathers said that wasn't enough. That God needed a man to make a commitment one way or the other. Like marriage.

Blake squirmed against that notion. He much preferred the idea of wide-open land and a life free of any real attachments. That had been his way since the night of his twelfth birthday, when he'd snuck out of the storeroom of the Gold Nugget saloon, where his mother had worked for as long as Blake could remember. He had been back once—three years later, only to discover his mother had died of an unnamed disease with his name on her lips. He'd left St. Louis forever that day, and joined his first wagon train, lying about his age and somehow convincing the wagon master that he was a scout. It was only dumb luck that Sam Two Feathers took a liking to him. Barely five years older, Sam had been a scout for two wagon trains west already and was making a name for himself as the best on the frontier. Sam was the only friend he'd ever had.

But there was no time to ponder the weighty thought any longer as the sound of boots crashing through the woods alerted him to the wayward men returning from town. They staggered toward the wagon train, and Blake knew they were more than a little drunk. These men would be lucky if they remembered their own names. He gripped his pistol but kept it holstered for the time being while he met them head-on.

"A little late, aren't ya, fellas?"

Willard stepped forward with his familiar conciliatory grin. "Lost track of time, Tanner. Won't happen again." His liquored breath wafted over Blake, turning his stomach, but Blake kept his face stoic and didn't show his revulsion. "This all of you?"

"Sure is." Again, that smile. Blake wasn't moved. But was relieved that all six were accounted for. That would save him the trouble of kicking anyone out of his train. For now, anyway.

He nodded toward an open area just beyond the wagons. "Best make camp outside of the circle tonight," he said.

"What do you mean?" A strapping farmer that Blake recognized as a newlywed, Barnabas Shewmate, seemed to sober up a bit.

"I'll not have drunkenness inside the circle of wagons." Blake eyed Willard, then shifted his gaze to the other family man, Zachary Kane. "Especially around the children of this train. Every last one of you heard the rules of the wagon train when you signed on. I can't keep you from drinking outside of camp, but I'll be hanged if I let any one of you men cross the wagon line."

Zach had the good grace to drop his gaze and look ashamed of himself, as did Barnabas. Willard tried on another grin, completely unashamed by his present state. "Aw, Blake. You ain't seriously suggesting we sleep on the hard ground when a couple of us got soft women to snuggle up against?"

Blake scrutinized the man, but again he remained like stone. "I'm not suggesting anything. I'm telling you flat out you're not getting any closer to the wagon train than this spot, until morning. Now, am I going to have any trouble out of you? Or are you going to take this like men and sleep it off out yonder?"

Willard's face clouded, eyes narrowed, and Blake tightened his grip around his Colt. Willard noted the movement, eyed the revolver, and backed down, but not before Blake noted a fire of hatred shooting from the man's dark eyes.

Relief that he'd avoided the possibility of a volatile incident sifted through Blake. He wasn't afraid to press his point, but he'd rather not have to use force. Making enemies was never a smart way to go if it could be avoided. As part of the wagon train, this man could possibly stand between him and death someday.

Blake could feel Willard's eyes on him as he walked back

to the wagons and instructed the night guards to make sure not one person except for Two Feathers entered the camp that night.

Blake couldn't help but have a sinking feeling that he and Willard would be coming to blows long before they reached Oregon.

Three

A twig cracked somewhere behind Fannie, causing her legs to halt even as her heart quickened its pace. If there was one thing she'd learned over the past three years, it was to keep her senses tuned in to possible danger. And right now every instinct told her someone had been following her since she left the mule-headed wagon master.

She figured she had a couple of choices. Run, which probably wouldn't do any good, or make a stand. Show her pursuer she might not be able to fight him off, but no way would she be caught unawares and without a fight. Stooping, she snatched a rock from the hard ground and slowly turned, summoning bravado she was far from feeling. "I know you're there," she called out. "Show yourself, you lily-livered coward."

The bushes behind her rustled. Fannie raised her arm and took aim.

"Wait! Fannie," a husky, slightly panicked female voice called out. "It's me, Toni. Don't throw the rock."

Fannie shoved out a breath and dropped her arm, nearly faint with relief. "Mercy, Toni, you scared the life out of me."

"You didn't seem scared." The blonde moved into the open, her body scantily clad and shivering in the coolness of the spring night. "As a matter of fact, I'd wager any man would have thought twice before attacking you."

The praise felt good. Fannie had to admit it, but there wasn't time to dwell on things like that. Tonight there was too much at stake. "What are you doing out here?"

"Following you. What did Mr. Tanner say?"

Fannie flung the rock against the nearest tree with all the pent-up force she could muster. "That man is a stubborn mule, and I hate him."

"I take it you couldn't convince him to change his mind?" Toni's voice sank with disappointment.

"No."

The prostitute's chest rose and fell, bespeaking a frustration that Fannie felt in her own heart. "What are we going to do?"

Fannie scowled. "We?"

She nodded and sashayed forward. "Neither of us can do this alone, Fannie. But together, we might have a chance to leave this godforsaken territory."

"I'm not alone. I have Kip and Katie."

Giving a shrug, Toni nodded her concession. "All right. So you don't need me. But I can't do this alone."

"What makes you think you need me?"

"I don't have a wagon. You do."

Fannie's hands went cold. "What are you talking about?"

Her voice trembled. How many folks knew her secret? Her gut tightened with the premonition that she needed to get home to Kip and Katie. Were the twins in danger? If this Toni—a woman she knew only by reputation and recognition—knew her biggest secret, did Tom know as well? What if he'd hurt the twins and was just waiting for her to get home? She turned on Toni with fury. "What do you know about a wagon?"

Her face, illuminated in the glow of the moon, hardened with determination. "Let's just say, the smithy is a regular client of mine, and he talks in his sleep."

Fannie's face burned with embarrassed indignation. "In his sleep, my eye. That lousy talebearer, Hank Moore. He swore he wouldn't tell anyone about my plans. I've got half a mind to—"

"Simmer down. Hank never came right out and said he was helping you. I'm good at putting two and two together when men need to feel important."

"I just bet you are," Fannie spit.

Toni's eyes narrowed, and she stepped closer. Standing inches taller than Fannie she might have been intimidating if Fannie hadn't been filled with her own desperation. Still, her voice trembled when she spoke. "I can't go back to town, Fannie. George will kill me if I do."

"What'd you do?"

"Besides running out on him in the first place—and since I'm late reporting for work, he's figured it out by now—I snuck into his room and took my money from his locked box." She gave a rueful smile and answered the next question before Fannie could ask. "I know where he keeps the key. I guess he never thought I'd have the gumption to go after my money, so he never hid it from me."

"Your money?" Fannie sniffed her disdain. "Does he know it was your money, or are you a stinking thief?"

Toni gave her a pointed look. "I earned every penny and more. It's rightfully mine."

Fannie's thoughts went back to her own stash of denied payment that she had taken from Tom. Her anger cooled. Perhaps she had more in common with this woman than she cared to admit.

"All right. Stay here. I'll come back and get you later tonight."

"I can't stay here like a cornered animal. George is going to be sending Arnold after me once he figures out I'm not just a bit late to work. I need to be somewhere Arnold can't find me."

Many times, Fannie had seen George's girls after his thug Arnold had finished getting them in line. Puffy lips, bruised faces. They never even tried to hide the wounds. How many times had Tom seen the fear in her eyes and threatened to make use of Arnold's services should she become too outspoken?

She could only imagine Toni's anxiety. "All right. Go to the old barn about a mile south of here. The wagon's hooked up, waiting for us. We'll be leaving in the night, soon as Tom's passed out drunk."

Toni nodded. "Thank you. You won't regret letting me come along."

Fannie grabbed her arm. "Give me your money."

"What?"

Holding out her hand, Fannie leveled a gaze at her new travel companion. "Let's just say, I don't want to open that barn and find my wagon and you gone when I get there."

Toni drew herself up with a dignity that might have been comical if not for their desperate situation. "I'm no thief." But she handed over her money just the same.

Fannie gave a snort. "Tell that to George."

"I already told you . . ."

"Shhh." Fannie's senses alerted her to the swish of body against bush.

"What?" Toni whispered.

Fannie silenced her with a raised hand and cocked her ear toward the sound. Perhaps an animal? They waited as minutes passed. Fannie's heart pounded violently in her ears.

"No one's there, Fannie," Toni hissed.

"Maybe, maybe not."

"It was probably a squirrel or rabbit or something."

Fannie nodded, not convinced, but if their pursuer wasn't going to reveal himself, what other choice did she have but to move on. She tucked Toni's money into her waistband. "Be careful heading to the barn. I'll be there as soon as we can get away."

The young woman reached out and embraced Fannie in a quick hug before she could step away. "You be careful too."

Fannie watched Toni leave until night and foliage covered her form. Then Fannie turned her attention back to the mile she still had to walk. It was later than she'd intended. No doubt Tom had been home for several minutes. Perhaps longer. Images of Kip and Katie in trouble began to torment her, and she quickened her pace until her footfalls came at a run.

If only they could get through one more evening of Tom's drunken raging, his gluttonous smacking, his filthy desires. One more night. And then they'd never have to endure him again.

When Sam Two Feathers stole back into camp, Blake didn't even bother to hide his curiosity. "What happened?"

"A woman followed the girl."

"A woman?" Surprised, Blake gave the scout all of his attention.

Sam nodded, squatting down in front of the fire as he reached forward and ladled beans into a tin plate. "A fancy woman, I think."

Bile sprang to Blake's throat. He knew exactly the fancy woman to whom Sam was referring. "What was she doing?"

"Ran away from someone named George. She wants to travel with the one named Fannie. They're going to meet up later when the girl can get away."

"Thunderation." Blake slapped at his thigh. "I told Fannie she couldn't come with us."

Sam shrugged. "I reckon she's not the kind to take no for an answer." He looked up and grinned. "Has her a wagon hid away somewhere. The fancy woman's hiding out there. I think they're coming whether you say they can or not."

Blake gave a huff of frustration. What was he going to do if she insisted on following the train?

As if reading his thoughts, Sam swallowed down a bite. "Might not be a bad idea to let her join us. She knew the woman was following her. Even picked up on my tracking. She has some real good instincts. Better than most men, I'd say."

"You know the rule. Even if I was inclined to bend it a little for the girl and her brother and sister, I'm not letting a saloon girl anywhere near this wagon train. Who knows what kind of trouble having a woman like that could cause."

"Maybe none."

"I'm not willing to take that chance. There are too many impressionable men and jealous women in the group. A fancy woman, even one trying to change her ways, can only cause trouble. I just don't need someone like that dirtying up my wagon train."

"Now, Blake, you know what the Good Book says."

Blake blinked. Sam knew he didn't have a notion what he was getting at.

He scowled and Sam smiled. "All right you don't know. It says that all have sinned and come short of the glory of God." Sam's sharp hazel eyes glowed like the sea in the firelight. "The woman is trying to find a new start. You would keep her from accomplishing that?"

"I'm not keeping her from anything but making trouble on my wagon train. You know as well as I do that it would only be a matter of weeks, maybe days, before she'd be practicing her profession."

By the light of the fire, Blake noted Sam's jaw clench. He knew the conversation was over. Sam wasn't much of one to push his thoughts off on another man. And no matter how strongly he might feel Blake was wrong, he wouldn't bring it up again. Blake knew that.

Relief washed over Fannie as she stepped breathlessly through the private entrance into the one room at the back of the store that served as Tom's living quarters. Katie stood over the stove. Kip sat at the table. She rushed into the room. "Tom's not home yet?"

Fear shot to Katie's eyes and, too late, Fannie realized her mistake. From the corner of her eye she saw Tom's meaty arm before she felt the blow. "Think yer gonna steal from me and run away?" She looked up from the ground, and despair washed over her. He held the bag of money. Her money. Escape money. New start money.

His heavy boot landed on her back, preventing her from rolling away. Tom grabbed her hair, reared back, and slammed her face into the ground. She heard Tom's roar of uncontrolled rage just before welcome blackness invaded her senses.

Fannie woke with a start to the unpleasant splash of ice-cold water on her face. She could taste blood and knew her lip was busted. And that wasn't all. Every inch of her body screamed in pain. A groan rose from her throat. With great effort, she opened her eyes.

"That did it." Kip's voice broke through the pain and cold, bringing Fannie fully conscious. "Come on, Fannie. You have to get up. Them ropes ain't going to hold Tom for long."

Ropes? "What happened?"

"Kip knocked him out cold," Katie said, her sweet voice

filled with pride. "Got him all tied up." She clutched the money bag.

Struggling to sit up, Fannie took note of the cast-iron frying pan slung on the floor and looked around until she spied Tom, sprawled on the floor. "Is he alive?"

Kip gave her a scowl. "Yeah. But I shoulda done him in after what he did to you."

Fannie followed her brother's gaze to the fat storekeeper. Her tormentor. His shirt had slid up, revealing a hairy, bloated stomach. Revulsion shook her.

"Does it hurt much, Fannie?"

"Yeah. Real bad." Her head, her back, her ribs. There was no point in lying about it. Katie and Kip had each been on the receiving end of Tom's fury, so they knew the pain that accompanied the blows.

Tom groaned and shifted.

Kip was right. Those bindings wouldn't hold for long. She had two choices. Run now, taking the chance that he'd be loose in moments and come after them before they could get away. Or take some time to tighten the ropes, despite her distaste at the thought of getting any closer to Tom than absolutely necessary. She made a quick decision. "Kip, go into the store and bring some more rope. Katie, bring me a square of cloth to tie around his mouth. We need to make sure he doesn't get away for at least a day." Hopefully the lazy drunk would decide they weren't worth the trouble of running after. The twins went their separate ways, and Fannie rose painfully to her feet.

"It ain't gonna do you no good to do this, gal."

She jumped, expecting the blows to begin again. But when she whipped around, she found Tom still tied up, struggling against his bindings. Yet panic bolted through her. Ignoring the stabbing pain in her sides, she grabbed the skillet and raised it over her head, ready to bring it down. "Fannie, NO!" Toni rushed across the room and reached for the skillet.

The opening door, accompanied by Toni's shout, brought Tom's head up. He noted the skillet, and terror shot to his eyes. With a screech, he shrank back like the coward he was. "Dear God in Heaven, make her stop!"

Fannie clutched the skillet tighter as Toni tried to muscle it from her fingers. This was her chance to be rid of him forever. But even now, staring into his mean, nasty face, she knew she couldn't do it. Not with Mama watching from Heaven.

Slowly, she relinquished her grip. Toni breathed out loudly. "Goodness, Fannie. Have you taken leave of your senses? You would have killed him."

"Killing is too good for him."

"Maybe so, but he's not dying tonight."

Fannie clutched her ribs as she came to her senses, and the pain returned. "I thought I told you to hide . . ." She eyed Tom and lowered her voice, "You know where."

"I'm sorry, Fannie. I couldn't find the place."

A snort from Tom brought Fannie's attention back around to the disgusting man. "George has been looking for you, gal. Where ya been?"

Toni gave a haughty toss of her blond ringlets, refusing to answer.

"Cat got your tongue?" Tom baited.

Katie returned with a strip of cloth. She carefully avoided looking at Tom, but that didn't stop him from trying to lower her defenses.

"Katie-gal," he said. "You best git over here and let me loose. Now, I know a sweet little girl like you didn't have nothin' to do with this. I won't be takin' nothin' out on you. Alls you gotta do is untie my hands."

Everything inside Fannie screamed to yell at him to just shut up—or else—but her stomach churned, and fear kept her silent. It wouldn't take much for him to get loose anyway. With or without Katie's help. Terror licked her insides at the very thought of what he might do if he were to break free from his bindings before they got away.

Where was Kip with that rope?

Unable to get a response from Katie, Tom turned his attention back to Toni. "Now, why do you want to run away, sweetheart? You know George counts on you."

Toni's chest rose and fell, and Fannie could tell she was this close to letting tears spill down her cheeks. Fannie wished Kip had thought to gag the man as well as tie him up. But she didn't want to chance getting too close until the bindings were tighter.

"Say hello to Arnold for me while you can still talk, because once he gets hold of you, I'm thinkin' you ain't going to be talkin' to no one for a coon's age. Probably won't be workin' for a while, neither." Tom's dark gaze took in Toni's scanty attire.

Toni drew the shawl more tightly about her.

The exchange brought another concern. "Don't you have any real clothes?" Fannie asked.

The woman's cheeks bloomed, and she shook her head. "George wouldn't allow it. I guess he doesn't figure any of his girls will run away if we're wearing undergarments."

"Sounds like a right smart idea," Tom blurted. "Soon as I get outta these ropes, I'm gonna make you and Katie, here, do that very thing."

Katie's body began to shake. Anger burned Fannie. It was one thing for Tom to bully her. Quite another for him to try to intimidate poor Katie. She tamped down her own fear and swung around to face Tom. "You shut up!" Before he could recover from the shock of her backtalk, she turned to her little sister. "Don't worry, Katie," she said softly. "We're getting out of here just as soon as Kip gets back with that rope."

"You just keep on a-dreamin', gal." Tom's voice lifted with anger, and his breath left his body in huffs as he strained against his ropes. He glared at Fannie, shooting darts of hatred from his eyes. "I'm gonna kill you, ya know."

Katie gasped.

Toni stepped forward and placed an arm around the petrified girl. "Don't listen to him, honey. He's not getting out of those ropes."

"And you ain't gettin' out of this town dressed like a whore," Tom shot back.

As much as she hated to admit it, Tom had a point. The wagon train folk would rather take a burning arrow through the heart than welcome a fancy woman to their sacred circle.

Of course there was no guarantee that bullheaded wagon master would ever change his mind anyway. But with Toni dressed like that, there was no chance at all. And Fannie couldn't risk that this woman, or anyone else, might keep her and the twins from being as safe as possible in the middle of the vast wagon train. Fannie moved slowly across the dirt floor and entered the store just as Kip came back carrying a rope. "About time," Fannie growled, as her head spun with dizzy blackness. She took a few deep gulps of air to gain control.

"Sorry," Kip muttered. "The dadburn thing was on the top shelf. I had to climb to reach it." He frowned and searched Fannie's face. "You okay?"

"I'll be fine."

"Where're you going?"

She jerked her thumb toward the saloon girl. "She can't come along dressed like that. You and Toni get him tied up tight and stuff Katie's cloth into that fat mouth of his. I'll just be a minute."

In the back of the room hung four plain dresses, where they'd been hanging for over two years. Tom was convinced that he needed to carry ready-made items for the travelers—although Fannie had tried to warn him these pioneer women might buy ribbons, but they weren't likely to plunk down good money for a ready-made dress to get ruined on the trail. She'd received a hard smack for her trouble. It had been the last time she'd offered her opinion on business matters. Now, however, she was glad for his poor business decision. She yanked two from their pegs and slung them over her arm;

then, on a whim, grabbed two pairs of trousers and two men's shirts for herself. She didn't care what anyone thought of her. She wasn't going to be encumbered in heavy skirts over the next few months. Carefully, she undressed and slid on the new clothes. Then she walked back into the living quarters just as Toni gave Tom a smug grin and stuffed a piece of flannel into his mouth. The muffled sound of his angry curses filled the room as he struggled against the newly secured bindings.

"Fannie, you're wearing britches!" Kip's scandalized voice filled the small room. "That ain't right."

"Mind your own business, Kip. I don't care if it isn't right. My dress wouldn't hold up on the trail. And none of these are going to fit me."

"I think you look kind of pretty in those clothes," Katie said. "Could I have some too?"

Fannie gave the girl an affectionate smile. "I'm afraid there aren't any trousers even close to your size, sweetie. Mine are the smallest pair and even they're too big. See?" She pulled up her shirt and showed her sister the rope with which she'd belted the britches.

"What if my dress doesn't last?"

It wasn't the first time Fannie had thought of that. "I packed some dress goods in the wagon, so we can make you a couple of sturdy dresses. Don't worry."

"Are those for me?" Toni asked.

Nodding, Fannie carefully handed the gowns to Toni, mindful of the sharp pain in her sides. That stinking Tom had broken some ribs again. "Maybe one of these will fit you. Unless you'd rather wear the trousers."

A smile spread across Toni's face. "It's been a long time since I wore lady's clothing. I believe I'll stick with these. And thank you for being so thoughtful." She dropped her shawl, then took note of Kip's stare.

"Kip, get your eyes back in your head," Fannie commanded. "Gather your things together."

"I'll just go into the store to change," Toni said.

She returned momentarily, looking more woman than prostitute in the dark blue cotton dress that was a bit too snug but eminently more suitable than the undergarments she had been wearing. She held out her hand. "May I have my money back? There's no chance of me stealing your wagon now, is there?"

"I guess not." Fannie handed it over.

Toni peeled off a couple of bills and tossed them on the floor in front of Tom. "For the gowns. Even though they're not worth that much."

"Why'd you do that? He wasn't ever going to sell them anyway," Fannie said.

"Because, I've already told you, I'm not a thief."

"Suit yourself." Fannie sprang into action. "Let's go."

"Wait, Fannie." Toni grabbed her arm. "If we go like this, someone may come along, tonight even, and let him go."

Fannie considered her words for a second. She was right. "What do you think we should do?"

Toni planted her hands on rounded hips and pursed her lips in concentration. Then she nodded. "We'll put a sign out front that Tom's gone to Council Grove for supplies. That way no one will look for him for a few days."

"What if he starves?"

Fannie gave a short laugh and motioned to his enormous stomach. "He could live for months on what's already in there."

"Fannie . . ."

"All right, fine." She shook her head. "But we can't say Council Grove. No one will look for him for at least a week if we do that."

"Good!" Kip spit.

"No, Kip. It's one thing to let him go without food, but if he doesn't have water, he'll die. And I don't want to stand before Mama's God and have to explain my part in that."

At the reminder of their ma's saintly ways, Kip nodded and dropped his defiant gaze. He kicked at the floor and shoved his fists into his pockets. "We'll just say he went huntin' for a few days."

"No one's going to believe that," Fannie said. "Everyone knows Tom couldn't shoot a dead deer at three feet, let alone bag a live animal."

A shrug lifted Toni's shoulders. "Kip's suggestion is best. Maybe it'll at least give us a day or so head start."

"All right." Ignoring the bruising pain in her shoulders and ribs and the excruciating ache in her head, Fannie grabbed a writing slate and pencil from the shelf below the counter and scratched out a note: Gone Hunting. Back in two days.

There. Anyone could live without food and water for a couple of days. Maybe when someone finally came looking for him, Tom would be too weak to come after her. That might buy them even more time.

Four

The sun peeked through wispy eastern clouds with brilliant streaks of red and blue promising a good day for the travelers to resume their journey. The camp was already beginning to stir as Blake returned from the creek after a cool, early-morning swim. They'd only been camped for one full day and one full night, but the pioneers had seen everything the town of Hawkins had to offer—such as it was—and most were anxious to move on, so even children were up and helping to pack up supplies.

The smells of sizzling bacon and fresh coffee wafted to his nose, and his stomach juices began to flow, demanding his full attention.

By the time he reached his fire, Sam greeted him with a tin cup filled with steaming coffee. He tossed him some jerky. Blake took it with rueful thanks and dropped down for a minute to consume his breakfast. "One of us has to learn how to cook, Sam." Usually it didn't matter. Women were the same everywhere, and married women couldn't bear the sight of an unfed bachelor. But on mornings such as this, when everyone was bustling about to get ready to move out, they were sometimes forgotten in the shuffle. Deer jerky had to serve as breakfast and right now he was grateful to have it.

Sam bowed his head and said a quick blessing. When they opened their eyes, Edna Cooper stood next to their fire holding two tin plates filled with bacon, eggs, and biscuits. "I thought you two might want a decent breakfast before we move out."

"Ah," Sam said with a grin as he accepted the proffered plate of food. "Something to truly give thanks for."

A pretty blush tinged the young widow's cheeks and rose to her blond hairline. She handed Blake his plate. The look she gave him could only be described as waiting. Searching. Blake smiled his thanks, careful not to brush her hand as he took the food. "That was thoughtful, Mrs. Cooper. Thank you."

"My pleasure, Mr. Tanner," she said without a touch of coquettishness. "I couldn't let you work a long day without a proper meal."

Blake stared at the food, at a loss whether he should respond or if it was okay to start eating. One look at the slab of bacon, and the big orange yokes on those eggs, and it was all he could do not to dig in.

Did she intend to stand there watching them eat? Awkward silence thickened the air. "Well," Edna finally said, "I suppose I should get back and see if Miles is finished." She gave a pleasant laugh. "I declare, that boy can eat like a grown man."

"Thanks again, ma'am," Sam said around a bite. "We'll bring back your plates in a few minutes."

She nodded, cast a last lingering look at Blake, and scurried away.

"Nice lady."

"Don't start," Blake warned.

"Okay."

"Any new wagons show up?"

"A couple."

Blake's heart jumped. "Oh?"

"Not her, though."

Shoving a bite of dripping eggs into his mouth, Blake sent him a scowl. "Her, who?"

A grin tipped his friend's lips. "The redhead."

Sam knew him too well. He hadn't slept much, worrying about that girl. No telling what she might do. Following the train could be dangerous. Any outlaws or Indians bent on mischief would pick off a lone wagon first. Still, if they hadn't shown up yet . . . well, forget the disappointment he felt . . . maybe the girl had wised up and decided to stay put where she belonged. "You think she's in some kind of trouble?" he asked his friend.

Sam's gaze remained fixed on the campfire. His eyes narrowed in thought. "Could be."

Condemnation squeezed Blake's heart. Dadburn it. He should have let her and her brother and sister join the train.

"Want me to go out and look for her?" Sam's tone was carefully noncommittal, but there was just enough of a knowing shift in pitch to raise Blake's ire, bringing him back to his senses.

He shoveled in the last of his bacon and shot to his feet,

still chewing. He swallowed down the bite with a swig of coffee. The fire hissed as he tossed the remains of his cup into embers. "I'm a wagon master, not a headmaster. I don't have time to look after a bunch of young'uns. We best finish breaking down camp and move out."

He wanted to put as much distance between Hawkins and the wagon train as he could, as quickly as possible.

Fannie woke with a start to the nauseating combination of manure and sweet-smelling hay. The sun shone brightly through the cracks in the barn and streamed into the opening in the canvas of the wagon, where they'd spent the night. The brightness stabbed her eyelids with the familiar pain of after-beating headache. Stretching was out of the question with the pain in her sides. And her shoulder hung from her body with stubbornness, so stiff and sore that moving it nearly squeezed a cry of pain from her swollen lips. Mindful of the twins still sleeping around her, she remained silent through sheer force of will.

Voices rose from outside the wagon. A man's voice, mocking, menacing. Fannie's heart raced. Had Tom already been discovered where they'd left him, tied up and gagged on the floor of his home? She took a quick glance around the wagon. Kip was just beginning to stir, and Katie's angelic face registered deep sleep still. But Toni was gone.

She pressed closer to the canvas flap and pulled it back barely enough so that she could see what was going on outside. Toni stood face-to-face with a man Fannie recognized as Arnold, one of George's cronies and someone Tom had complained about losing money to in more than one game of chance.

"Leave them alone, Arnold. They're just kids." Toni's voice quaked. Fannie knew Toni had been on the receiving end of Arnold's brand of discipline at one time or another like the rest of George's girls, so she understood her fear.

Still, Fannie's emotions lifted with relief that it was Arnold and not Tom who had found them. But in the second after that thought, she knew how dangerous their situation had become. George's thug had beaten every fancy woman in town more than once and regularly tossed rambunctious drunkards out of George's tavern. Regret surged through her. She should have known better than to let Toni tag along. Tom would have been too stupid and too tied up to find them anytime soon. But Arnold . . . how could she have not considered Arnold?

"You sayin' you'll come back without a fight if I let Fannie and the twins go?"

Fannie held her breath.

"That's right."

An evil chuckle filled the barn. "I don't need your bargains. Yer comin' back either way. And so are them young'uns. I bet ol' Tom'll be willin' to pay a pretty penny to get them back."

Toni's voice shrilled as she called him a foul name.

A loud crack filled the barn as Arnold reared back and let his hand connect hard with Toni's cheek. She hit the ground before he pulled back his hand.

Fannie's own body still ached from last night's beating, but she couldn't sit by and let Toni go through the same thing.

Singed with anger, she started to reach for the flap. Giving no thought to her course of action once she came face-to-face with the thug, she could barely see through her anger. A hand on her elbow halted her. Kip pressed cold metal into her hand. Fannie's eyes widened as she looked down at the Colt. She hadn't even thought about them needing a gun.

She nodded her approval to her brother just as a rat-faced man poked his head inside the wagon. "Well, lookee what we have here."

Fannie shoved the barrel of the pistol inches from his nose. His eyes widened. "Hey, now. What's this?"

"Get back," Fannie said, mustering all of her courage.

"Now, you take it easy there, little gal. Do you even know how to use that thing?"

"You'd best get back, mister," Fannie warned, relieved that her voice held steady. "Or I might have to demonstrate just how straight I can shoot by putting a bullet in your head."

"Now, no need to be threatening." But he backed up, obviously not willing to call her bluff.

"Toni, grab his gun from his belt."

The saloon girl stood on shaky legs and did as she was instructed, obviously still a bit disoriented. Fresh anger washed over Fannie. Why did men just think they could beat on women all the time? "Take out his gun and keep a close eye on him. If he makes any quick moves, plug him."

"O-okay," Toni said.

With Toni covering Arnold, Fannie climbed from the wagon, catching her breath as a sudden sharp pain in her side nearly sent her into a swoon. She gathered herself together and shook off the dizziness. "You two stay put," she instructed the twins.

"Aw, Fannie. I could help," Kip said.

Fannie hesitated, then inclined her head. As much as she hated to admit it, she really did need the boy's help. "Do we have any extra rope?"

Arnold sent up a roar of outrage. "You think I'm going to let a bunch of kids and a whore tie me up?"

Fannie swung around to face the man. He wasn't the pathetic, drunken fool Tom was. His eyes glittered cold as ice. No. This man wouldn't sit by passively while they made their escape. Besides, now that he'd seen them, he'd go back and find Tom, hours before they'd planned. All the months and months of planning would be for nothing.

"What are we going to do, Fannie?" Katie's whisper-soft voice eked out of the wagon.

The sound of her sister's fearful question brought Fannie to a quick decision. She nodded decisively. "We'll have to kill him." She hadn't meant to speak the words aloud. But now that she had, she knew she had no choice. It was him or them. And she'd rather see him die than risk Kip and Katie going back to Tom.

"Now, just hold on a dad gum minute, little girl. You go right ahead and tie me up. I won't make no fuss."

"Fannie"—Toni's soft voice penetrated the barn—"killing is too good for him, I understand, but if you do this, you'll be no better than he is, or George, or Tom."

"Listen to her, Fannie," Arnold said, his voice beginning to tremble with fear. "You don't want to have my life on your conscience, do you?"

"You shut up," she said, waving the gun menacingly. "You hear?" Her mind swirled with possible scenarios. And none were pretty.

The barn door swung open, revealing a hulking shadow against the sun's brilliance. "What's this?" Hank Moore stepped out of the glare, with his gun drawn, and Fannie nearly fainted, so grateful was she to see him.

"Oh, Hank." Toni's relief was unmistakable. "Arnold is trying to take me back."

The smithy sent a cold glare toward the henchman. "Well, I reckon we ain't gonna let that happen."

Arnold's face turned to stone. "George ain't gonna like you helping his girl."

Hank ignored the other man and turned to Kip. "You shouldn't have kept the team hitched all night, son. But no matter now. Pull the wagon out and get the women settled in."

"Do as he says, Kip," Fannie instructed. "We've likely already missed the wagon train by a good three hours. We have some time to make up."

"What are you going to do?" Toni asked Hank. Fannie couldn't understand her worried tone. It was enough for her that the man had shown up just when they needed him. Whatever happened from here on out, at least they had a chance to get away before Arnold could make it back to Hawkins and spread the word that they'd gone.

"Now don't worry, sweetheart," Hank said, slipping his arm around Toni's shoulders while keeping his gun fixed on Arnold with his other hand. "I'm just going to have me a little talk with Arnold here. Once we reach an understanding, I'll catch up to you and say good-bye."

Fannie watched, deeply relieved that Hank had shown up and taken the question of what to do with Arnold out of her hands. Now all she could think of was getting away from the area before someone discovered Tom. She tugged on Toni's arm. "If you're coming with me, let's go. I'm not waiting one more second. We've lost more time than I intended by sleeping too long."

Toni's brow puckered. "Hank?"

He nodded toward the barn door. "You go like Fannie says."

The blacksmith's face gentled considerably as he looked at her. Fannie's breath cooled as she sucked it in. That man was in love with Toni. Well, that could only help them out. Maybe allowing the prostitute to come along would prove to be a blessing instead of a curse after all.

By noon, the town of Hawkins, Kansas, was largely forgotten as the travelers turned their attention westward, onward. Back to the routine of the trail. Even the six men who had tied one on at the saloon the night before seemed in good spirits, and there didn't appear to be any tension between the married men and their wives. Not that Blake would have blamed the women for being angry, but he couldn't help but be relieved not to have to mediate between feuding married couples. Especially when his own nerves were taut as he kept one eye on the wagon train and one fixed firmly on the horizon behind the train. By now, with no sign of the little scrap of a young woman, Blake was almost sure she'd given up and would try her luck with the next wagon train, which would most likely be coming through during the next month or so.

Only the barest amount of regret pinched at him as he firmly pushed aside the image of startling ocean blue eyes and riotous red curls. Besides, after that breakfast this morning, he'd practically made up his mind to redouble his efforts in Edna's direction. True, he wasn't in love with her, but he enjoyed her conversation, when he understood what she was talking about. She read poetry and such and enjoyed discussing it with him. But he supposed a man could put up with that nonsense for a woman who could cook like Mrs. Cooper. And he needed a wife. If he didn't speak up soon, he'd lose his chance. There were ten other men in the wagon train alone on the lookout for a wife before they reached Oregon.

"Here they come." Sam's voice broke through Blake's musings. He looked in the direction the scout pointed, and a grin tugged at his lips. All thought of Edna fled as, even across the plains, Fannie's red hair blazed like a roaring prairie fire.

His heart gave a leap. "Looks like you were right. She's not one to take no for an answer, is she?" Blake pulled his horse to a halt. "I think I'll ride out and greet them."

"What are you going to do?"

A shrug lifted Blake's shoulders. "I guess we'll find out in a few minutes."

* * *

"Someone's coming out to meet us."

Kip's announcement was unnecessary. Fannie had been expecting the wagon master's confrontation ever since they'd gotten close enough to the train to be spotted, and her gaze had remained fixed in that direction. She braced herself now. Determination squared her shoulders.

"Take it easy, Fannie," Toni said softly. "Don't antagonize him, or he'll never let us join them."

The admonishment raised Fannie's ire. "I'm not planning to antagonize him. He'd better not antagonize me either."

"Oh, Fannie," she said. "Let me do the talking, or your stubbornness is going to land us all right back in Hawkins or dead on the trail."

"Maybe she's right," Katie whispered, her eyes wide with fright.

Kip's freckles scrunched up as he gave her a deep frown. "Yeah, Fannie. Let Toni talk. You're just going to get that fellow mad."

Fannie looked around at the three worried faces and expelled a breath. Mercy, did they honestly think she was incapable of using her head? She knew the best way to get what you wanted was to smile and speak pleasantly. True, this fellow had a way of getting her irked so that she said the first thing that popped into her head, but she knew what was at stake here. "I'll do the talking. But I'll be civil."

Toni nodded, but there was hesitance in her eyes.

Fannie reached out and squeezed her hand. "I promise I won't risk our chances of joining the wagon train."

They fell silent as the muscled stallion pulled to a halt beneath the equally well muscled Blake Tanner. His gaze swept the group, then settled on Fannie. "Out for a little ride?"

Swallowing the sharp retort that was already forming on her tongue, Fannie stared at him, forcing a look of pure innocence. "We're headed west." She cleared her throat. "Same as you."

"I thought I told you no unaccompanied women on my train, Miss Caldwell."

"You made your position perfectly clear, Mr. Tanner. But I'm not traveling in your line of wagons. See? We're all the way over here, and you're way over there." Fannie gripped the reins with hands that were already smarting from two enormous blisters beginning to form on her palms. "We-uh-can travel west if we want to. There's no law saying we can't, is there?" Fannie mentally kicked herself. How could she have been dumb enough to mention the law when they'd just broken several of them?

"None that I'm aware of." His face remained statuesque as he kept his stern gaze fixed on her face.

Try as she might to read his expression, Fannie had no idea what might be going through his mind.

"Tell me, Miss Caldwell, do you take me for a fool?"

Fannie opened her mouth to answer but shut it again as Toni punched her in the arm. She drew as deep a breath as she could around the pain in her ribs and bit back the obvious retort, opting instead for a more conciliatory reply. "We don't want to interfere with your wagon train, Mr. Tanner. Nor do we wish our presence to cause you distress. But we have our reasons for wanting to leave Hawkins."

"I'm sure you do, Miss Caldwell. But you and I both know if you travel in this proximity to the wagon train, I will be forced to look after you."

Fannie couldn't resist a triumphant smile. She knew she shouldn't antagonize the wagon master, but she'd done well so far, and so briefly allowed for the upward curve of her lips. "We don't need anyone to look after us, sir. We'll stay on our side of the road, and you and your long wagon train may stay on yours."

He scowled, and Fannie felt her courage fail her. What would she do if he ordered her to take an alternate route? Could he do that?

"Miss Caldwell," he said, with the rise and fall of his chest, "you've left me no choice but to include your wagon with the rest. You will travel somewhere in the middle in a designated spot that my scout, Sam Two Feathers, will show you."

"Yippee!" Kip's outburst nearly sent Fannie out of her own skin, but she couldn't blame him. She, too, felt like jumping for joy.

"Don't think you've won, Fannie."

She jerked back to look at Blake, only to find his stern brown eyes penetrating hers. She fought the urge to look away guiltily. Instead, she met his gaze head-on. "I didn't know it was a contest."

He ignored the comment and shoved his finger toward her. "Let this be the last order you disobey," he said. "Is that clear?"

Orders? Oh, no. She was through taking orders. Especially from men. She gathered in a deep breath, ready to give the wagon master a good piece of her mind, when Toni's hand touched her arm, and the prostitute spoke, forcing Fannie to release her breath without benefit of releasing her onslaught of words. "Mr. Tanner. We appreciate your reconsidering. We promise not to be any trouble."

"See that you aren't, or, trust me, I won't think twice about forcing you to leave at the nearest town." Though his words were in answer to Toni's comment, he spoke directly to Fannie.

A soft cough came from Katie, reminding Fannie just why she was so determined to join the wagon train in the first place. And she made a decision. She would not force this man's hand. Rather, she'd be a model passenger. She forced a smile she was far from feeling. "I won't disobey again."

Five

Blake hid a grin at the girl's oath. He was almost positive Fannie wouldn't be able to keep her promise not to disobey his orders. But for now he was willing to give her the benefit of the doubt and hope for the best. Besides, something wasn't quite right. Fannie's mouth was swollen as though she'd been knocked around. Her cheek was bruised, and, unless Blake was mistaken, she seemed to be moving slowly and with deliberate moves. There! Another wince.

"What happened to you?" he asked, surprising himself with the gruffness of his question.

Fannie looked up, surprise parting her bruised lips. "Are you speaking to me?"

"Who else?" He peered more closely. "You've been knocked around pretty good, if I had to guess."

Her face grew stormy, and she sniffed, but turned away. "Then don't guess," she said flatly. "I appreciate your letting us into your train. For the twins' sake, but how I got these bruises is my business."

Blake had always figured people had the right to keep their own affairs private. But something about this young woman drew his curiosity; more than that, his blood pumped with outrage that anyone could bruise such a beautiful face, or in any way try to break this young woman's indomitable spirit. Sure, she was probably one to provoke a man to frustration, but to lay a hand on her? He'd like to get his hands on the fella who did this.

"All right. Keep it to yourself. But the safety of all these people, including you, rests with me. So if you're in any trouble that might follow you here, tell me now."

Her hesitation was all Blake needed. "Yes?"

"I simply don't know, Mr. Tanner. The man I'm running away from might come after me. And Toni is running from the man who owns the saloon." She gave him a fierce frown. "We have a right to leave. It's just that some people want to keep us against our will."

Call him a fool, but he believed her. "Then let's hope they let you leave in peace."

Two Feathers gave him a nod of approval as he escorted the newest members of his wagon train back to the long line of travelers. It only took a few minutes to reposition the wagons to tuck Fannie and her little group into a good spot directly in the middle. As Blake rode away, he noted that her face had relaxed for the first time since he'd made her acquaintance the day before.

His own muscles let go of the tension between his shoulder blades. He had a feeling that whoever had knocked Fannie around wasn't going to just lie down and allow her to walk out of his life. As much as he dreaded the inevitable trouble to come on account of that girl, he didn't have to worry about her anymore. Now he knew exactly where she was, and he would be close by if she needed him. Fannie Caldwell needed looking after whether she knew it or not.

"Stop that crazy cow before she causes a stampede."

Blake's command shot through the air, and he galloped by without a glance in Fannie's direction. After one full day and night on the trail, Blake still hadn't bothered to speak a word to her, so she averted her gaze just to prove she didn't care if he had forgotten her existence.

"Now that is one fine-looking man."

Toni's words slammed into her gut like the butt of a rifle. Fannie clamped her lips together and refused to acknowledge the swift shot of jealousy.

"Don't you think?"

"No."

"Oh, come now." Toni's voice chimed with knowing amusement. "Every female from ten to a hundred is watching that man ride down the line."

"Not me." Fannie had to force her eyes forward as the urge to gawk nearly won in her inward battle of wills.

"Fine, have it your way, Fannie-girl." Toni laughed. "But you aren't fooling me one bit."

Fannie couldn't help but allow herself the memory of Blake riding by. She admired the way he sat on a horse. Confident, commanding, able. If he'd ever crack a smile, he would have reminded her of her pa, but of course, Pa was a gentleman given to laughter and fun. Fannie couldn't imagine Blake tossing back his head in laughter. Well, maybe she could imagine it for a second. A swift image of his lips curved in a smile, his throat moving in laughter caused a leap in her stomach.

Stop it! she told herself in no uncertain terms. Thoughts of Blake Tanner were strictly prohibited. Strictly. She would not be one of those swooning fools like that Edna Cooper who Fannie had noticed walking beside her wagon up ahead. The young woman seemed to find every excuse to call to Blake. To draw attention to herself. And Fannie had noticed the young woman leaving her campfire with two plates of food this morning at breakfast. Later, she'd watched Mr. Two Feathers return the tin plates empty. It didn't take too much to figure out that Mrs. Cooper had set her cap for the handsome wagon master. And she was more than welcome to him as far as Fannie was concerned.

"Get her for the love of . . ."

The whole wagon train howled with laughter as a wayward heifer broke loose and evaded the men trying to rope her.

Toni snickered. "Not wranglers are they? I hope these men plan on farming in Oregon."

The thunder of hooves came their way. Straight toward the wagon. Fannie's head already spinning from the pain of sitting all day driving the oxen, she couldn't even imagine trying to jump out of the way of a scared cow on the run.

"Yee haw!" Fannie swung around just in time to see Kip jump from the wagon right in front of the animal.

Shoving the reins in Toni's hands, Fannie forgot her pain and shot up from the wagon seat. "Kip!" But it was too late. She watched in horror as he waved his arms just like he'd lost his mind.

Terror bolted through her, beginning at her head and traveling all the way down her body, weakening her knees. She knew the boy was good as dead. But in the beat of a heart, a miracle happened. The cow just stopped. Still. Nose to nose with Kip.

Fannie looked on in silence, her voice not catching up with the scream that had been rising to her throat just a split second earlier. Kip reached out and scratched the cow's head between her eyes. The cow's owner, Mr. Markus, ran forward and slipped a thick rope around her neck. He reached out and ruffled Kip's hair. "You done good, boy."

Blake rode up. He looked down from his mount like a king on a throne and gave Kip a stern frown. "That was rather foolish, don't you think? What if she hadn't stopped?"

Kicking at the dust, Kip shrugged. "I don't know. I just figured she would."

"Look at me, son."

Kip did as he was told for once and bravely met Blake's gaze.

"What you did was brave. I admire you for that. And I can't deny that I'm relieved that stupid cow got caught before she did any real damage to anyone's property. But do you realize how dangerous your stunt was?"

"I guess so," Kip mumbled.

"You guess so? Look how worried your sister is."

Fannie drew a sharp breath as the attention shifted to her. How could Blake do that? Tears she hadn't even known she was shedding flowed down her face. She wiped them away with a quick swipe.

Kip swallowed hard, and remorse showed on his face. "I'm sorry, Fannie. I just wanted to stop that ol' cow."

Embarrassment combined with the rush of realizing he'd narrowly escaped death was too much for Fannie. She scowled at him. "That was the dumbest thing you've ever done, Kip Caldwell. Mama and Pa are likely turning over in their graves about now thinking how you almost joined them."

Blake cleared his throat. "Well, let's just be glad he's all right. And, as punishment for this stunt, you'll have extra duty for the next two weeks." He turned to the half-Indian scout. "What do you think, Sam? Should he join you hunting and scouting?"

Fannie watched in outrage as Kip didn't even try to hide his elation at his so-called punishment.

Sam nodded soberly. "I could use a strong young man to help."

"That okay with you, Miss Caldwell?"

Fannie was on the verge of spouting her opinion of what sort of disciplinarian he was when she realized what he was doing. He was taking Kip under his wing. Giving him a chance to focus his impulsiveness in a positive direction. She blinked hard against a rush of fresh tears. For a second she could have happily thrown her arms around the infuriating wagon master and thanked him over and over. Instead, she sat abruptly and nodded. "That's fine."

Blake turned to Kip. "Can you ride?"

"I-I don't have a horse, sir."

"That wasn't the question."

He gave a short nod. "I used to ride, but haven't since my ma died, and Silas sold the horses."

"Kip," Katie hissed, reminding him that they didn't share their personal life.

Blake seemed to have the matter well in hand. "It's all right. I have two extra horses. You can borrow one of mine."

"Thank you, sir!"

"I hope you have a sore behind for a month," Fannie muttered.

"What was that, Miss Caldwell?" Blake asked.

"Nothing."

Four other wagons had joined the train in Hawkins, so they were over a hundred wagons—four hundred passengers and then some. Maybe closer to five hundred. An enormous undertaking for a wagon master. But he had several captains overseeing sections of wagons. Trusted men he felt would lead with fairness as well as a firm hand. Edna's father-in-law, Vern Cooper, was in charge of the section of train Fannie had joined.

Thanks to Mr. Markus and his unruly heifer, they had reached the creek later than expected and thus were late making camp. But that didn't seem to bother the travelers too much. Seemed like the first few days after a stopover, they were anxious to push on a few extra miles and eat a later supper. And Blake was happy to oblige. But he, too, fought against a thick layer of trail dust and an overabundance of fatigue. He was more than ready to stretch out on his bedroll for a few hours of sleep. But several more hours of work loomed ahead of him and everyone else in camp. Wood was scarce in this part of Kansas, so buffalo chips must be gathered to make fires. Details of women and children to assign for drawing water from the nearby river. Meals to prepare for that evening, animals to tend to. This time of day, the relief of stopping was soon outweighed by the backbreaking work that followed.

Blake rode Dusty, his brown stallion, down the line, watching as wagons were unhitched and oxen were set loose to graze freely within the large circle of wagons.

"Hello, Mr. Tanner," Toni called, as he passed the new wagon, carefully keeping his gaze fixed with only cursory interest. The kind he reserved for 99 percent of his wagon train. Toni's bold call sent a tremor of resentment through him. Lest she harbor the mistaken notion that he had changed his mind about her presence, he gave her the most curt of nods, then turned his focus to Fannie, who seemed to be struggling with the oxen. He frowned as he looked closer and noted her grimace.

Without even thinking about whether it was a good idea or not, Blake pulled Dusty to a halt and swung down off the horse's back. He stalked to Fannie's side. "Need some help?" he asked.

"No," she grunted, struggling with the yoke.

"Where's Kip?" he asked. The boy would only be riding scout and hunting during the day. At camp he had other chores to do. "Shouldn't he be helping with the heavy work?"

Immediately, Blake knew that was the wrong thing to ask. She jerked her chin up, shooting blue daggers through him with her eyes. "Mr. Cooper, your *captain* sent him out looking for buffalo chips."

Blake nodded. "That's what the children of the train do while the men take care of unhitching their teams."

She gripped the bar, and Blake caught sight of her palms. He sucked in a breath as blood smeared onto the leather harness.

"Move aside, Fannie. Let me help you do this."

"No thank you."

Blake gave a frustrated grunt. "Suit yourself." He stalked back to Dusty and rode away. That was the most stubborn . . . Only after he was more than ten wagon lengths from her did it occur to him that she had in fact disobeyed an order, thus breaking a promise that was less than ten hours old.

Toni set a pot of coffee on the fire to boil and scowled at Fannie. "Honestly, Fannie. Your hands are nothing more than raw meat, and no matter how tightly your ribs are bound, you have to be in terrible pain. I can see it all over your face. You should have let Mr. Tanner help."

"How can you defend him after the way he snubbed you?"

It wasn't easy. Toni had to admit it. No matter how many years had passed since she'd been received by decent folks, she still struggled with the humiliation of being treated as though she were no better than an alley rat. It hadn't taken long on the trail to realize that enough people recognized her that she wouldn't be able to hide who she was. A fresh start seemed out of her reach. Even the wagon master couldn't bear the sight of her. Couldn't acknowledge a friendly greeting without that suspicious, disgusted look she'd seen in so many eyes over the years. Still, her concern wasn't for Mr. Tanner but for Fannie.

"I don't care about his feelings, Fannie," she said. "I care about your pain."

Tears sprang to Fannie's eyes. "It doesn't hurt so much."

Compassion shot to Toni's heart, and she placed her arm around Fannie. "Katie brought a bucket of water from the river. Why don't you go give those hands a soak in some salt water, and I'll take care of the oxen."

Fannie gave a snort. "What's a saloon girl know about unhitching a wagon?"

Without taking offense, Toni took Fannie firmly by her slender shoulders and pulled her away from the oxen. "As much as you do, I'll vow. I wasn't always a saloon girl. Once upon a time, I was a simple farm girl from Missouri."

Ashen-faced, Fannie placed a swollen hand on Toni's arm. "I'm sorry."

"Don't be." Toni smiled what she knew was not a very convincing smile. "That part of my life is over forever. We're going to the promised land."

Sam Two Feathers hung back and watched the two new women. He had a gleeful feeling Blake Tanner might just have met his match in Miss Caldwell. But it was the other woman who caught Sam's interest. No matter what Miss Toni might have been in the past, it was obvious she was ready and willing to work hard now. She struggled against the oxen, but eventually got the team unhitched. He smiled at her victory and wondered how anyone could be that beautiful.

"Why didn't you go help her?" Sam turned at the sound of Blake's irritated tone.

"She needs to learn to do it herself."

"A woman like that only needs to know how to do one thing."

Sam shook his head, pushing down his own irritation. "Not this woman. She is good. Wants a fresh start. She's ripe for God's picking."

"Mark my words—no man will marry her, and she'll be signing on with one of the brothels in Oregon before the new year."

"I do not think so." He couldn't take her eyes off the white-blond hair flowing effortlessly in the breeze. "This woman is determined. She will starve before she sells her body again."

Blake clapped Sam on the shoulder. "You just go on having faith in folks that don't deserve it, Two Feathers. But I'll not be fooled by a conniving woman. And you'd best not get any ideas about that one. She's not good enough for you."

In silent reflection, Sam watched his friend walk away. Blake stubbornly refused to suffer so much as a glance at Fannie's wagon. But Sam couldn't keep from turning back for one more lingering look at Toni. She pulled the oxen forward and slapped them each on the behind, sending them off to graze safely away from their fire.

She nodded at a passerby, head high with the pride of a

person who has just accomplished a feat. Sam's own heart swelled, pleased for her. No matter what Blake thought, this woman was one of quality and substance. Sam knew he had no right having those sorts of thoughts about a woman like Toni. Not because she wasn't good enough for him as Blake had said, but because the pairing of a white woman and a half-breed Sioux, wouldn't be overlooked among decent folks, any more than would Toni's previous occupation. But at least she could hide her occupation. His high forehead and hawklike nose, along with sleek black hair and a brown complexion, left no doubt in anyone's mind as to his heritage. And Sam wasn't ashamed of his Sioux blood, but he had to admit choosing to live in the white world had been a lonely choice. Blake was his only friend, and no white women would give him a second look.

But he knew God had a purpose for his life. Felt sure there was a woman out there handpicked by God just for him, and Sam was willing to wait for however long it took to find such a woman.

Fannie fought back tears as salt water penetrated the open blisters on her hands. "It hurts bad, Fannie?" Katie asked, her wide blue eyes liquid with compassion.

"Not too bad," she lied. "Just stings a little."

Kip stomped back into their camp. "I ain't doing that again, Fannie."

Fannie fought against pain, fatigue, and frustration. She had little compassion to spare for Kip just because he found his chore of gathering buffalo chips degrading. "Well, Kip. You heard what Mr. Tanner said about obeying orders," she said matter-of-factly. "So you'll either pick up buffalo chips like you're told, or we'll get kicked out of the wagon train."

Kip scuffed the ground with the toe of his boot. "Aw, who needs these folks anyway? We can make it on our own."

She removed her hands from the salt water and shoved her bloody palms at him. "Can we?"

The insolence left his face as soon as he saw the wounds. "I can take care of the wagon and oxen. You gather buffalo chips. Okay?"

"Oh, that's a wonderful idea, Kip." Katie's face brightened into a smile of admiration at her twin.

The thought of not having to fight with the stubborn animals was awfully appealing to Fannie. And Blake had mentioned discussing the possibility with the captain charged with assigning chores in their section of the wagon train. But she had no intention of admitting she couldn't handle a pair of dumb oxen. "Those aren't the chores we were assigned."

Kip shrugged, and his expression once again twisted into rebellion. "What difference does it make as long as the work gets done?"

The boy had a point. And the thought of not having to fight the pain and dizziness of pulling against the animals appealed to her a great deal. "All right. Maybe it won't matter so much as long as the chores are done. Tomorrow evening, I'll join your detail while you unhitch the oxen and start the fire."

Relief softened his expression. Then another look Fannie couldn't quite decipher.

"What?" Fannie asked. "Why the look?"

He shrugged. "How come you been acting so different?"

"Different. How?"

His eyes turned stormy, accusing. "You promised Mr. Tanner you'd obey his orders. And I've never seen you act like you can't do hard work, but you've been favoring your sides. You hurt or something?"

Heat rose to Fannie's cheeks. "I made that promise just so Mr. Tanner wouldn't kick our behinds all the way back to Hawkins, Kip. We have to be smart, and if that means pretending to do as we're told . . . then . . ."

"Just like with Ol' Tom."

"Exactly." They had to do as they were told on the outside and do whatever they needed to do when no one was looking. They had survived that way for three years. They could do it for a few more months, until they reached their new home. "So you understand, now. Right? You have to do as you're told. Don't make trouble. Soon as we get to Oregon, we'll be on our own, and no one will ever tell us what to do again. Okay?"

"Mr. Two Feathers is gonna teach me how to hunt and scout. That might come in handy for when we get to Oregon."

Fannie's strength was finally fading, and she smiled wearily. "That's good, Kip. Real good."

Kip's freckled nose creased between his eyes. "You hurt, Fannie?"

"Yeah. Tom did a real number on me this time. Sometimes I can't breathe."

His eyes clouded with worry. "Think we ought to ask

around and find out if there's a doc in the train?"

Fannie shook her head with sudden vehemence. "No. Kip. Listen to me. We can't make any trouble. If Mr. Tanner finds out I'm hurt, he'll make us leave the train sure as anything."

"I don't know, Fannie. He seems a decent sort of man. It ain't your fault you got the stuffing knocked out of you."

"Isn't. You know better than to speak improperly. What would Ma say?"

"What difference does it make?" he asked, his freckles popping out with defiance.

"I don't know, Kip. But Ma always wanted us to speak properly. She said it set the quality folk apart from the ignoramuses. Do you want to be an ignoramus?"

"I guess not. But I still don't think it matters where we're going."

"Well, just remember Ma and mind your grammar."

Before he could answer, nausea suddenly hit Fannie, and panic rose as she looked around for someplace to retch. She barely made it behind the wagon before becoming sick.

Pain sliced through her ribs each time she heaved, and her breath came in raspy gasps. "Fannie?"

Fannie's head swam, and she grabbed for the wagon wheel to keep from crashing to the dusty ground, as her throat closed, and she began to lose consciousness for the second time in as many days.

Six

Blake paced outside of Fannie's wagon while Sadie Barnes looked Fannie over with a carefully trained eye. He could have kicked himself for not making sure they had a doctor in the train this time around. Even more, he kicked himself for being so shortsighted. How could he have not seen that Fannie was injured so badly? He should have insisted she be honest with him when he first noticed her bruises.

Toni handed him a steaming cup of coffee.

He took it with a jerk of his head. "Thanks," he muttered.

"You're welcome." She gave a shaky breath, and Blake could tell she was just as worried as he was.

Sadie appeared through the opening in the canvas cover on Fannie's wagon.

Blake rushed forward, slopping coffee on the back of his hand, but he barely felt the sting. "Well?"

"Help me out of this contraption," the middle-aged widow snapped.

Blake extended his hand and provided support as the plump woman climbed from the wagon.

"Well?" he repeated.

"The poor girl took a beating. Didn't you notice?"

Blake stiffened at the accusation in her tone. "I noticed someone had fattened her lip and bruised her cheek. But I didn't want to pry. And she didn't offer the information." As a matter of fact, she'd told him in no uncertain terms to mind his own business.

"A fat lip and a few bruises on her face are the least of her injuries."

"What do you mean?"

"The girl's body looks like she's been stampeded by a herd of buffaloes." She shook her head, her brown eyes flashing with anger. "One big black-and-blue bruise. Broken ribs. She's a mess. That's for certain."

Guilt squeezed Blake's heart. "Are you telling me she's been driving that wagon and working nearly two days with those injuries?"

Mrs. Barnes nodded grimly. "That's what I'm telling you, Mr. Tanner. If I had to guess, I'd say she's accustomed to taking a beating and pulling herself together in time to work like a dog. But this time, she's likely made herself worse. And if you have a decent bone in your body, you'll see to it that she rests for a few days and gives her little body a chance to heal."

"You mean call a halt?" Blake's stomach dropped, and he blinked like a fool. Only a woman would even think of stopping a whole wagon train for one person. He'd be more likely to send her back to Hawkins and go on without her.

Apparently, Sadie recognized his bafflement for what it was. She jammed her hands onto her hips and gave him the deepest frown he'd ever seen. "Well, we wouldn't want to do anything to throw off your precious schedule, would we?" Her lips dripped with sarcasm. "Especially for a slip of a girl like Fannie."

Now, comments like that were uncalled for. He was responsible for the welfare of over four hundred people—all of whom had put their trust in him to see that they arrived at their destination in one piece. He couldn't take a chance that an early snow season or a harsher-than-usual winter might blow in and catch them unawares.

Still, he didn't want to be unreasonable. He glanced at Sam. "What do you think?"

The scout shrugged. "It's up to you. We've already lost two days stopping for repairs."

That was Sam's way. Present the obvious and allow Blake to come to his own decision. Raking his fingers roughly through his hair, Blake looked across the horizon as if searching for answers from the tall prairie grasses waving in the early-summer breeze. But no answers were forthcoming.

"Mister?"

Blake turned at the sound of the little angel-faced sister. The girl's appearance was similar to Fannie's but not so freckled, not so wise, not so hard. Blake crouched down until he met the child's sad, worried eyes. "Yes?"

"Fannie took an awful beating."

"Shut up, Katie!" The brother gave the girl a shove, sending her sprawling to the ground, her eyes wide with surprise as she scrambled to her feet in the next second.

Springing into action, Blake grabbed the boy by the scruff of his neck. "Never lay your hand on a female, son."

The boy's eyes blazed with anger and rebellion. Not even an ounce of remorse softened the steel in his face. "We don't air our dirty laundry, mister."

"Now you listen to me." Blake let the youngster go, but commanded his attention with a firm tone. "Your sister is injured and needs to heal for a couple of days before we move forward."

Anger gave way to fear in the lad's eyes. "We got to get more distance between us and Hawkins, or ol' Tom'll find her and give her the same again. He might even kill her this time."

What on earth had this family been through? Compassion rose in Blake. He realized his decision had crept up on him without his even realizing. He glanced up at Sam. "Inform each captain we'll be staying in camp for two days."

Sam nodded and silently left to carry out the order.

Katie's sweet face melted into relief. But Kip's scowl remained in place.

Blake clapped the boy on his shoulder. "Don't worry, son. We'll keep an eye on your sister and make sure no one harms her."

"The only thing we wanted from you was to keep moving." The distrust remained firmly planted around the freckles. "I'll make sure no one hurts my sister. She ain't your concern."

"Then stay close to her and don't let anyone come around the wagon. You're on guard duty." Blake studied the young man's face. "You man enough?"

Thin shoulders squared with the weight of responsibility. He nodded solemnly. "I'll keep my sister safe."

"Good." Blake turned to Sadie. "Keep me informed on how she's doing," he said.

"She just needs a couple of days to rest, and she'll be fine. Still sore for a while, but past the point of danger from the jostling wagon."

He nodded to Toni, figuring it was the least he could do. After all, she was worried about Fannie too. "I'll be back later," he said. He turned and mounted Dusty.

"Wait, Mr. Tanner."

Dread hit Blake's gut. He should never have been pleasant to Toni. She'd expect conversation and well wishes and possibly more. He hardened his gaze as he looked down from his seat atop his horse. "What can I do for you?"

"Kip had a point. There's a good chance Fannie could still be in danger. We told you that in the first place."

Blake knew she was right. He'd walked right into this situation with his eyes wide open. He had no one to blame but himself for including the little group in the train. Now he had no choice but to fulfill his duty as wagon master and see to it that Fannie's injuries didn't become life-threatening, which they very well could if she didn't give those ribs a chance to heal. "We'll do our best to keep Miss Caldwell safe. Leave the train's security to me."

She stiffened under his reprimand. Her lip curled, and her eyebrow lifted. "And yet you left Fannie's security to a twelve-year-old boy."

Heat rose to Blake's cheeks. He wasn't used to criticism and chastisement, least of all by a woman like this. "I know what I'm doing."

"I'm not worried whether you do or not. It's Kip I have my doubts about. The boy is a hothead."

"Good day, Toni," he said, without bothering to acknowledge her concern or tip his hat as he would a decent woman. Blake whipped his horse around.

"He has a gun," she called after him. "And he's been itching to use it. You think he was impulsive to jump in front of a charging cow? Wait until he pulls a gun and shoots without taking time to consider what he's doing."

Blake's heart went cold at the image her words evoked. She had a point. The boy without a weapon had almost gotten himself killed. With a gun? Blake shuddered to think of the consequences.

But he didn't give her the satisfaction of returning to investigate her claims further. Rather, he kept the information at the forefront of his mind and headed back to his campfire.

Fannie woke slowly to the soft glow of moonlight streaming in through the canvas opening at the back of the wagon. The sweet smell of sunflowers and clean air wafted to her, and she tried to drink in the fragrance. A sharp pain shallowed her breath, and she let out an involuntary moan.

Toni sat up from her pallet. "Fannie?"

"How long was I asleep?"

"At least twelve hours. Mrs. Barnes gave you laudanum for the pain. Mr. Tanner called a halt for a couple of days while you heal up enough to move forward."

"He knows?"

"Not everything. Katie told him you'd been beaten."

Anger shot through Fannie. "Katie knows we don't—"

"Air your dirty laundry," Toni provided. "Kip made that abundantly clear, but it was too late, and Mr. Tanner already knew."

"We can't stay here like dead ducks. We haven't put enough distance between us and Hawkins."

Toni gave a solemn nod in the darkness. "I know. But Mr. Tanner has made up his mind. He's not going to give in. You know how stubborn he is."

Fannie glanced around the wagon. Katie's eyes were closed in sleep, her long eyelashes sweeping rosy cheeks. She sighed and rolled over onto her side.

"Where's Kip?"

"Standing guard."

Fannie sat up quickly and cried out as sharp pain sliced through her torso.

"Take it easy, Fannie." Toni's hand pressed against her shoulder. "Lie down. Kip's fine."

"What's a boy doing standing guard for a wagon train?" What could Blake be thinking? "Are they that short of men?"

"Kip asked to watch over our wagon. Mr. Tanner allowed

him the dignity of doing so. I told him about Kip's gun."

"Good, then he'll keep an eye on him." Fannie felt herself starting to fade out. "Could you go check on Kip and make sure he's warm enough?"

Toni pulled the comforter more closely about Fannie's shoulders. "You get some rest. I'll check on Kip."

Fannie was asleep before Toni reached the opening to the canvas. Toni glanced back, affection surging inside of her. All these years she'd buried any hope of growing attached to anyone, yet now, within just a few days, this family of orphans had taken root inside of her heart, igniting fiery loyalty and something very close to familial love. She stepped outside, as promised, and found Kip sitting, gun in hand, against the wagon wheel. His head drooped, his chest rising and falling in telltale sleep.

She started to reach out, but a hand on her arm startled her. A scream tore at her throat, muffled by a swift hand across her mouth. "Do not be frightened, Miss Toni," came a soft voice next to her ear. "It's Sam Two Feathers."

Toni relaxed and gave a nod of understanding.

The Indian scout lowered his hand but put a finger to his lips. "He may become startled if you wake him. I don't want him to come out of sleep and start shooting."

"I see your point," Toni whispered.

"Why are you outside?" he asked. "Everything okay?"

"Fannie woke up and asked me to check on Kip. I promised I would." She shook her head. "He should be inside asleep with his sisters."

"The boy has much to learn." Two Feathers focused on

Kip's form. "Keeping his word is the most important lesson."

"His word?"

The scout gave a short nod. "Standing watch."

Honestly, Toni had to wonder about men such as Blake and Sam. They seemed to be part of a rigid honor system that extended to each person from infant to the grave, with no exceptions. "He's just a child. Surely, you don't expect him to stay awake all night and guard his family's wagon like a grown man."

"I do." His jaw tightened with determination. "And so does Blake. Survival depends upon each person doing his duty, and doing it well."

Kip stirred and jerked awake. Two Feathers nodded. "Good," he whispered. "Only a couple of minutes went by. His sense of duty awakened him. He'll be a good man someday."

Sam's hand, warm on her arm, was beginning to feel confining, and panic rose inside of Toni. She pulled her arm away, and Sam immediately let her go.

"Do not worry, Miss Toni. You are well guarded. Kip will not fall asleep again."

"How can you possibly know that?"

A smile touched the corners of his lips. "He's discovered that he has a weakness and is ashamed of himself. He won't allow himself to fall asleep again."

Toni warmed to his gentle smile, then, suddenly aware of how close she was to this man, pulled back. What if someone saw her in the dark with a man and got the wrong idea? She had already felt the condemnation of a few of the women on the train. They knew who she was. Within another day or two, her former profession would be common knowledge. All the more reason for her to keep her distance from men.

Sam couldn't keep his eyes off the woman. Her white-blond hair fascinated him more than he'd like to admit and beckoned him with its silky shine. As much as he wanted to summon the strength to turn away, it was impossible. He watched her slender form, waiting for her to disappear beneath the white canvas covering.

He caught his breath as she turned just before entering the wagon. "Good night, Mr. Two Feathers," she whispered.

Before he could recover enough to respond, she had already ducked inside.

Sam's insides lit up, like a Roman candle. A crazy grin touched his lips as he turned—just in time to feel a blow to the side of his head. Blackness hit him just as he realized he'd let down his guard and now Toni, Fannie, and the twins were in danger.

Seven

Blake stretched out fully on his bedroll and stared into the vast expanse of a starlit night. The beauty of such a moment could be shared with someone special, but never explained. Even the most eloquent poet couldn't capture the magnificence of a prairie sky on a clear night.

A deep sense of peace settled over Blake. This would be his last train, and at the end of the trail, after years of delivering hundreds of pioneers to their land of promise, it was finally his turn to settle.

It was his turn to build a life, a home, a family of his own. He'd been eyeing some of the single young women in the train, Edna in particular. Not seriously, but taking stock just the same. Might be smart to stake his claim and find a wife before all the men out West started speaking up. The ratio of men to women was three to one, and if a man went west without a ready-made wife, it was only the luck of the draw whether he'd find one or not.

He knew the kind of woman he wanted. Someone soft,

sweet, kind. The sort of woman a man could look forward to finding at home after a full day of working in the fields. A woman he could count on for a nice meal, a hot cup of coffee, and a well-kept home. And eventually, a passel of young'uns, boys mostly, to help out on the farm and carry on the name of Tanner. Edna's boy, Miles, was a strapping lad, four years old, polite, and smart. So Blake knew she was the sort of woman who would provide the children he longed for. That was his dream. He'd been saving almost every penny he'd earned over the past five years. Within a few months he could hang up his wanderer's hat and begin building his life.

Crack.

Instinct yanked Blake from the ground to his feet before his head registered the sound of a rifle fire. He snatched his Colt from its holster next to him as he stood. Men were already starting to come out of their tents and wagons before he had passed three campfires. He had to find the source of that shot before things grew chaotic. Where in thunderation was Sam?

His feet led him toward the first place that flashed to his mind: Fannie's wagon. A high-pitched, child's scream split the air, and he knew he was headed in the right direction. Blake increased his speed until he reached his destination. A group had already gathered by the time he arrived. He elbowed his way through the bystanders and stopped short at the sight of Katie, gripped in the meaty hands of a man of enormous girth. Her small body shook with fear, and tears poured down her cheeks.

"What's going on?" Blake demanded. He knew he had to

tread carefully. This man could snap Katie's neck without any effort whatsoever.

"Nothing you need to worry about, mister," the man snarled.

Fighting against his sudden anger, Blake knew he had to maintain control of what could turn into a volatile situation. But there was no way he was letting this man kidnap Katie or anyone else. "Let's just pretend it *is* something I need to worry about. What are you doing manhandling that little girl?"

"Like I said"—the man kept a firm hold on Katie's bone-thin arm and moved forward—"it ain't none of your never mind. But just so's there ain't no trouble, this girl and her brother and sister is indentured to me."

"It's not true," Kip said, pulling against the other man, tall and bald, with the longest neck Blake had ever seen. A gun flashed against Kip's side, but the apparent danger didn't seem to deter the boy in the slightest.

The fat man's face reddened in anger. "You callin' me a liar, boy?"

"That's what you are," Kip spit back.

The man turned to Blake with a cajoling smile that showed a gap where his two front teeth had once hung in his mouth. The grin only boiled Blake's blood.

Katie found her voice. "D-don't let him take us back, Mr. Tanner."

The man shook her arm, making her whole body vibrate with the movement.

"Shut up," he growled before looking back at Blake, clearly tired of making the attempt at civility. "I paid me fifty dollars fair and square to their pa. Now hand Fannie over to me, and we'll just be headin' back to Hawkins."

Movement from the wagon behind them caught Blake's attention. Pale and trembling, Fannie appeared at the canvas opening. "Don't believe him, Mr. Tanner," she said, gasping with pain.

Blake stepped forward and extended his hand, half-assisting, half-carrying Fannie down from the wagon. "Are you saying this man doesn't have a right to you and the twins?"

"That's exactly what I'm saying."

"Lyin' scrap of a gal. You know dern well I paid for you fair and square."

Fannie turned angry eyes on the man, but even in the protection of Blake's arm, she trembled in fear. It didn't take much deduction to figure out this man had been the source of the beating she'd received.

"If Miss Caldwell says you're lying, I'm inclined to believe her, mister. I suggest you and your friend release the children and leave the way you came. We don't want trouble."

"Now, lookee here, mister." He dropped Katie's arm, and the little girl ran to Fannie, burying her head in Fannie's side. Blake dropped his arm from Fannie's shoulders and braced himself for what could turn into an ugly incident. He knew there were at least six members of his wagon train with rifles pointed at the two intruders. But if he could resolve the matter without gunfire, without bloodshed, he would prefer it. Still, he figured it was this man's choice.

"I said, I don't want trouble," Blake said, giving the man a cold, even glare. "But if you want some, I'll be happy to oblige."

"All I want is what's mine."

"I'm not letting you take these three without proof they belong with you."

A look of pure stupidity slid across the man's face. "What kind of proof you talkin' about?"

Was this man as dumb as he appeared to be? "Indentured servants enter into a contractual agreement. Do you have a document proving your claim?"

A frown creased the wide forehead. "You mean a piece of paper sayin' I bought 'em?"

Indignation formed a black shadow across Blake's heart. "You can't buy children in this country. Not white children anyway."

"Mr. Tanner?" Fannie's weak voice spoke up once more. "He paid my stepfather fifty dollars to keep us indentured for two years."

"There," the fat man said with smug self-assurance. "She admitted it."

Blake frowned and turned to the young woman. "Fannie?"

She shook her head. "He's kept us as his slaves for three years. The way I figure, he owes me a year's salary."

From outside the wagon circle, a limb snapped. They turned as another stranger entered the camp, pistol drawn and cocked. "The girl's right."

"Hank!" Toni finally spoke up. "What are you doing?"

The woolly man looked familiar, but Blake couldn't quite

place him. For now anyway. He knew it would come to him eventually.

"Miss Toni," he said, "I saw these men ride out and figured they was up to no good."

The man still holding on to Kip gave a snort. "Shoulda knowed you'd be behind this, Hank." He turned to the fat man. "That fool smithy's been sweet on my girl for years."

Smithy. Now Blake remembered why he looked familiar. The man was the town of Hawkins's blacksmith.

"I'm not your girl, George. I worked for you," Toni said, her voice cracking with nerves. "I'm free to leave Hawkins if I choose."

The man's eyes glittered dangerously, and he leaned closer to her. Toni shrank back even though she had to know there was no real threat with six men ready to plug this fellow should he make one false move.

"I think we've heard enough." Blake turned to the fat man. He was barely able to keep from punching the sweating pig of a man. "Fannie clearly has no obligation to you any longer. And Toni has made it plain she doesn't intend to return to Hawkins, so I suggest you men clear out."

"We ain't clearin' outta nowhere without what belongs to me."

"We don't belong to you, Tom. We fulfilled our obligation a year ago." Fannie's face was pale, and even in the firelight of the lanterns held by several of the bystanders it was pretty clear she was about to faint. "I'm not taking my Kip and Katie back to that stinking town no matter what. So you might as well do as Mr. Tanner said and clear on out of here."

Without a word, the man moved with surprising speed, hauling his enormous frame toward Fannie. She sidestepped, as though accustomed to the move, and he lunged forward, narrowly catching himself before plunging headlong into the wagon.

Sam finally showed up, looking disheveled and in pain, but holding his Colt out in front of him. "Mister, if you know what's good for you, you'll take that advice."

Tom glanced around, finally realizing he was badly outnumbered and outgunned. "Let's go, George."

George shoved Kip forward. He glared around at the group of at least fifty that had gathered in the commotion. He pointed a filthy gnarled finger at Toni. "You ain't never gonna be any better than what you are, Toni. You was nothing when I found you. Hungry and skinny and half-dead. This is the thanks I get for taking you in and savin' your life?"

Shaking her head, Toni met his angry gaze head on. "*Thank* you? You made me what I became. But, no more. Do you hear me? Never again."

He sneered. "You ain't never gonna be no more than you are, girl. And that's a fact."

Hank Moore stepped between George and Toni. His eyes glittered dangerously as he stared the man down, heedless of the six-shooter in George's hands. "You heard the wagon master, George. It's time for you and Tom to go."

"You'll be sorry, Hank. You know she ain't never gonna care for you like you care for her. Ain't you spent enough on her?"

Hank said nothing, and finally George spun and walked

toward a red sorrel mare. He swung himself into the saddle and galloped away without a backward glance. Hatred glittered in Tom's eyes. Blake braced himself for trouble. Surely the fool wouldn't try anything stupid. Tom looked from Fannie to Blake, indecision clouding his simpleminded expression. "You going to cause trouble, Tom?"

At the sound of Blake's veiled threat, Tom finally made up his mind and backed down. He hauled his girth to his poor horse's back, the man's behind so large the saddle was hidden beneath his layers of fat. Disgust rolled through Blake as he watched the two men ride away.

He spun on Sam. "I thought you were supposed to be looking out for them."

Giving a humble nod, the scout raked his fingers through shoulder-length hair. "I was distracted and didn't hear them. They jumped me and knocked me out cold."

"They did?" If Blake had known that, he wouldn't have let them off so easily. "You okay?"

"Head's a mite sore. But I guess I'm none the worse for wear. Nothing a good night's sleep won't cure. Unless you want me to keep watch again?"

Blake gripped his rifle. "No. I'll stand guard over Fannie and the rest."

"I'll stand guard over my own wagon," Kip growled, thrusting out his chest and rising to his full height.

"I take it you're the one that fired a shot?" Blake eyed the lad.

"That's right."

"Good job. If you hadn't alerted the wagon train, they

would have snuck in and stolen all of you away, including Toni."

The boy beamed beneath the praise. "Weren't nothing much," he mumbled.

"It was. And I'm glad to know I can count on you to look after the women. But you have a full day ahead of you keeping watch and attending to your chores. A boy your age needs plenty of sleep so your bones will grow."

Kip's eyes squinted with distrust. "What about you? You don't need sleep?"

The kid had a point. And a sharp mind. Blake liked that. "As someone who is much older, I've slept years longer than you already. I'm better suited to lose a little sleep. Besides, I'd feel better if you're watching over your sister from inside the wagon while I look after the outside."

Kip's eyes brightened with understanding. "Yeah, if ol' Tom gets past you, he's going to have to deal with me."

Blake's lips twitched. "Exactly."

"If you two have it all worked out," came Fannie's weak voice, "I'm going to say good night."

"Kip, climb up ahead of your sister," he instructed. Kip did as he was told.

"Put your arms around my neck, Fannie."

"Not in a million years, mister," she said, her stubborn bravado shadowed by the weakness of her words.

"Aw, Fannie," Kip said. "Do as he says."

"Mind your own business, Kip," she said, her voice so soft, Blake feared she'd pass out any second. "I don't need his help."

"Well, you're going to get it anyway." Without waiting for permission he knew would never be granted, he swung her tiny body into his arms. Inches from her face, he looked into her eyes. Up close, they were even more alluring than from a distance, and Blake couldn't help the ideas swarming his mind. Only her weary sigh brought him back to reality and kept him from making a fool of himself. As carefully as he could, he lifted her into the wagon bed while Kip took hold of her to keep her steady.

"Thank you, both," she said, clearly in pain. "Good night."

Blake turned to Toni. She seemed to read the request in his eyes, for she came forward. "I'll take care of her, Mr. Tanner."

"Thank you."

She nodded at Sam. "Good night again, Mr. Two Feathers. Take care of that knot on your head."

An embarrassed smile quirked Sam's lip. "I will, Miss Toni."

"Good night, Hank," she said to the smithy. "Thanks for coming to the rescue again."

The burly blacksmith squeezed his battered hat between his beefy hands. His face cracked into a smile. "My pleasure." The canvas flap lowered behind her, leaving Blake and Sam to break up the gathering of onlookers. "Morning's coming awfully early, folks," Blake announced. "I suggest everyone turn in for what's left of night."

Willard stepped forward, smiling his usual mocking grin. "Mighty chivalrous of you protecting those women and the young'uns."

Blake's defenses rose. "Chivalry had nothing to do with it. I would have done the same for you."

"Still, a man has to wonder if trouble's going to keep following us now that those four are part of the train."

"You just concentrate on not causing trouble of your own, Willard, and I'll worry about Miss Caldwell and Toni. Got it?"

Blake left him standing and strode to where Hank Moore still hung back, watching the wagon. Blake extended his hand, taking note of the other man's strong grip and work-hardened palms. "Thanks for your help, Hank."

The giant of a man inclined his head. "Glad I was handy."

"What are your plans now?"

"I ain't goin' back to Hawkins, thet's for sure," he said. "You-uh-got room for another man on horseback?"

This could be the answer to one more problem for the wagon train. A smithy would be an invaluable addition. "You're a blacksmith, right?"

"Yep."

Blake exchanged a look with Sam, expecting to find easy acceptance. Instead, hesitance clouded the hazel eyes. Concern slid through Blake; it wasn't like Sam to stand in judgment of anyone.

Still, without a good reason, how could Blake say no? Especially after the man had given up his life in Hawkins to watch over Fannie and Toni? That action alone deserved the benefit of the doubt. "We can always use a blacksmith. As long as you keep prices fair."

"You got my word on that."

"You can put your bedroll next to my fire."

"If it's all the same to you, I'd rather stay close to Miss Toni's wagon so I can keep an eye on her. George ain't gonna give up just because you say so."

"As a matter of fact, it's not all the same to me. It's not proper for you to sleep outside of her wagon. I'm sure Toni doesn't need the train's gossip mill to buzz any more than it already will after the truth about her past came up tonight. And if I'm not mistaken, one of those men actually implied you're a longtime customer."

The man's eyes caught fire, and Blake braced himself just in case the fellow might take a swing.

"Mr. Tanner?"

Blake turned to the sound of Kip's voice coming from the wagon. "What is it, Kip? Everything okay?"

"You ought to let Mr. Moore stay outside our wagon. He helped us get away from Tom. Even kept our wagon and oxen for us. We wouldn't be here if he hadn't helped us out. Couldn't you just sorta let folks know that Mr. Moore ain't doin' anything improper? Miss Toni's changing her ways. I heard her say so."

Blake hesitated at the youthful ability to believe in folks. He considered the lad's words. It would be nice for someone else to assume responsibility for the women and young'uns. He surely didn't have time to play nursemaid to the bull-headed Miss Caldwell and her wagonload.

Again Blake looked at Sam for approval, and again he was greeted with hesitance. He knew he'd have to get Sam alone and find out what it was about the blacksmith that made his friend's hackles rise.

"The boy might feel safer if someone he knows and trusts stays outside the wagon, Mr. Tanner," Hank said. In the firelight, Blake took note of a look in Hank's eyes that might have been desperation. The man must really care about Fannie and the twins. Still, he couldn't just dismiss Sam's concerns without at least taking time to investigate further.

Never one to let another man think for him, Blake shook his head. "I'll stand guard tonight. You're welcome to join me. I could always use the company."

The smithy's eyes grew dark, and he seemed about to argue, but a sudden change came over his face as his gaze landed on Kip. He smiled at the lad and ruffled his red hair, which was in desperate need of a pair of shears. "There, you see?" he said with the tenderness of a father. "You'll be safe with Mr. Tanner standing guard. And I'll be here too."

Kip's face relaxed into something akin to relief. "Good night, Mr. Moore," he said. "I'm glad you decided to come with us. When Fannie wakes up, she'll be glad too."

The man's expression softened beneath his bushy beard. "Me too, son."

Blake watched the paternal exchange with a sense of foreboding. The man seemed to be a savior. But Blake had never known Sam's instincts to fail him, and that gave him more than a little reason to pause. On the other hand, he'd seen the way Sam looked at Toni. Could his reservation be a simple case of the basest of human emotion? Jealousy? The only other time Sam had been wrong about a man had also involved a woman. And that time almost got him killed. Sam might be a brilliant tracker and the best shot in the West, but when it came to women he was about as dumb as one of Fannie's oxen.

He walked away from the wagon, where Sam still stood, looking on like a mother hen watching over her chicks. "You best turn in," he said. "Morning comes early."

Sam shook his head. "Later." He stared at the blacksmith as the man made himself comfortable against a wagon wheel, his rifle laid strategically across his lap.

"Suit yourself." Blake knew better than to try to make Sam talk when he didn't want to. And right now, all his friend seemed to want was to keep an eye on the newcomer.

Blake headed back to the wagon, mentally shaking his head. Sam must be smitten with the prostitute if he was so determined to watch the man standing watch over the wagon. Blake knew from experience that Sam made his own decisions. If he'd decided this woman was somehow special, no amount of talking would convince him to look elsewhere for love. But he supposed he shouldn't judge. Being half-Indian, Sam's choices for a wife were limited. Most white women wouldn't look at him twice, let alone consider him a suitable match. But a woman like Toni . . . she ought to be grateful any man would even consider a relationship with her that lasted for more than an hour.

Blake listened to the sounds of the camp as folks settled back down after the upset of a gunshot and attempted kidnapping. He figured husbands and fathers would be restless at the thought of anyone wandering into camp and carrying off their loved ones. But he wasn't too worried. He didn't figure the two men would try anything more tonight.

From the looks of things, Fannie needed at least a couple days more to recover before they could move on. The laudanum was keeping her asleep, which was the best way for her to be so she didn't stress her body more than necessary. But he dreaded having to inform the wagon train they couldn't move forward because of one woman . . . a new member of the wagon train at that. No one would understand the delay.

Blake didn't quite understand his actions himself. He only knew that he couldn't leave Fannie behind and risk her being captured by that brute of a taskmaster. He could only imagine the abuses she had already suffered at the man's hands, even before the latest beating. And despite the repercussions, he couldn't move forward and take a risk she might be killed from the shaking of her wagon. The choice was clear . . . they would wait, even if that meant discontent and suspicion throughout the rest of the train.

George's Gold Nugget saloon buzzed with speculation. Where was Toni? For that matter, where was Arnold? The henchman hadn't been seen in a couple of days. Tom sat across from George, nursing a glass of whiskey, morosely imagining what he should have said. Done.

"Shoulda used my rifle."

George nodded. "Thet's whut we get fer tryin' to go in there nicely and appeal to those folks' sense of decency."

"Yep. Wanna go back?"

Guzzling down a beer, George let out an earsplitting belch and shook his head. "Naw, they ain't gonna let us nowheres near them women now."

"Know who I want to shoot?" His pickled tongue slurred the words. But he didn't care.

"Hank," George supplied.

Tom nodded and tipped his whiskey glass, flinching as the amber liquid burned his throat, then relaxing as it warmed his stomach, giving him courage to imagine himself walking into that camp and taking out whoever stood in his way. He slammed his fist on the table and shoved his girth back in his chair and stood on shaky legs.

"Whut do ya think yer doin'?" George asked gruffly.

"I'm goin' to git Fannie." He reached for his hat and missed, reached again and grabbed the battered covering.

"Sit down, ya dumb mule."

Quick anger shot through Tom. He was sick of folks calling him dumb, no-good, fat. He shoved the table into George. "I'm goin'."

George's face grew red, and he stood, his pistol in hand. "I said sit down, idiot. We're gonna stick to the plan. You remember the plan?"

Coward. They called him coward too. But looking down the barrel of a Colt revolver, Tom sobered up good and fast. He plopped his body back into the chair.

"We're gonna git them back. But we gotta be smart about it this time. Plan better so we don't walk away empty-handed."

George lifted the whiskey bottle and poured Tom another drink. That settled him right down. One thing about George, he wasn't stingy with his liquor.

The saloon doors swung open just as he reached for the

glass. Clay Robinson staggered in, carrying a man over his shoulder. Even before he tossed the man onto the plank floor, Tom knew.

"I found him in the old barn south of town. He's been dead for a couple a days."

Tom stayed put while George walked across the floor and stared down at his friend, the man who had done all of his dirty work for the past five years.

"Git him outta here, Clay," George instructed. The circle around the dead man thinned out. "I'll give ya a full day's wages to take him off somewhere an' bury him."

"Ya got yerself a deal," Clay muttered around a wad of tobacco. He hefted the dead man to his shoulder once more and exited the way he came. As though nothing out of the ordinary had occurred, the farmers, miners, and traders went back to drinking, gambling, and the saloon girls.

George walked back to the table and took his seat. He reached for his glass of whiskey and downed it in one swallow. "Well, now," he said, his face stone cold. "This looks like a case for the law."

"The law?" That was the last thing Tom wanted to see come to Hawkins. When a town got a sheriff, it got civilized. Before long a preacher would be building a church, and decent folk who looked down their self-righteous noses would move in and take things over. He couldn't abide that.

"Why do we need to call in the law? It ain't gonna do Arnold any good now."

George drew an impatient breath. "We just gonna let those women get the best of us? That wagon train's gettin' more and more distance on us. And before long, they's gonna be gone fer good. I figure only the law has a chance at bringin' them back."

"You think Fannie killed Arnold?" Tom knew well and good the girl was a lot of trouble, but if she was going to murder anyone, it would have been him. No. She was no killer, and Toni had refused to leave him long enough without food and water where he would die. "No. Fannie didn't have nothin' to do with it."

George nodded. "The way he's sliced up, I'd say Hank's huntin' knife did a number on him."

Tom swallowed hard at the cold assessment of the man's untimely death. A man who was supposedly George's friend. "Then how's that gonna get the girls back?"

Tom leaned forward, his gut squeezed uncomfortably against the edge of the table. "Well? How's Hank killin' Arnold gonna get my Fannie back?"

"We send the U.S. Marshal after the girls. Hank'll have to come forward and confess."

"Why'd a fellow do that?"

"Ya know how that fool feels about Toni. I'd bet my right arm he's all set to marry up with her and settle down out West like she weren't never no fancy girl." George summoned another bottle of whiskey from the saloon girl behind the counter.

Confusion that Tom attributed to the mind-numbing effects of half a bottle of whiskey clouded his mind, and he couldn't quite grasp the logic behind George's reasoning.

A chuckle rumbled the saloon keeper's chest. "I kin tell by

that dumb look on yer face ya ain't got no understandin' of whut I'm gettin' at." He took the bottle from the girl, smacked her on the rump, and chuckled again as she stumbled away.

No sense denying it when there was so much at stake. "Thet's right."

George popped open the whiskey and poured them each another tumblerful. "Trust me. By the time Toni and Fannie clear their names, the wagon train'll be long gone. And they'll be back." His eyes glittered with an evil that made Tom shudder. He wasn't sure, but he had a bad feeling he'd just partnered with the devil.

Eight

Fannie winced as the wagon wheels jerked over endless ruts on the well-worn trail. She had to admit today was better than yesterday, and yesterday easier than the day before. But she was growing impatient with her slow progress. They'd been back on the trail for a week now, and she was beginning to despair of ever getting her strength back.

Blake had instructed Mr. Cooper, the captain of their section, to assign her to fuel-gathering duty, so she, along with the children of the camp, gathered buffalo chips and small twigs where they could be found. Today would be her first day working the chore. She was ready.

"How you feeling?" Toni asked from her seat next to Fannie. Toni's hands gripped the reins. She'd learned to drive the oxen pretty well.

"Better," Fannie said. "But I'll be glad when Blake calls a halt for the day."

Toni glanced across the horizon toward the western sky. "Shouldn't be long now. Maybe another hour."

An hour could seem like an eternity. But Fannie was determined not to complain.

"Hi, Fannie." The sweet sound of Katie's voice reached her ears, and she looked to the side of the wagon. Her sister walked next to another little girl who Fannie didn't recognize. The strange child gave her a bright smile that wrinkled her nose and won Fannie over without effort.

"This is Becca Kane," Katie said. "They're a few wagons back. Her ma says I can walk with her if it's okay with you."

"Rebecca Marie Kane!" The stern sound of a woman's voice brought a look of guilty worry to the little girl's face.

She swung around. "Yes, Mama?"

The woman, a tall, slender brunette who was most likely around thirty years of age, stomped forward and took hold of her daughter's hand. "What have I told you about disturbing these . . . ladies?"

Toni bristled next to Fannie but, to her credit, didn't cause a scene in front of the children.

"Becca was just asking if she and my little sister could walk together." Fannie kept her steady gaze on the woman's face. "I was under the impression it was okay with you. But if it isn't . . ."

Mrs. Kane's expression remained firm, but she gave a nod. "Becca knows she may walk with the other children, as long as she does it close to our wagon."

"I'm sorry, Ma. Katie wanted me to meet Fannie."

Fannie slid from the slow-moving wagon and extended her hand. "I'm Katie's sister, Fannie Caldwell."

For the first time since her arrival, the woman's expression of steel softened, and she took Fannie's offered hand. "Amanda Kane. I didn't mean any offense. But one can't be too careful. She's all I have left."

"Your husband . . . ?"

"Oh, well, yes, my husband Zach. But Becca's my only living child."

Fannie didn't pry, but could see the pain of fresh wounds in the woman's eyes. "You can be sure I'll look after Becca anytime she wants to come to our wagon."

Hesitance creased her brow. "Thank you, but I . . ."

Fannie understood a little of what the woman must be feeling. She truly was happy to see Katie make a friend, but she wanted to keep her sister close. What if Tom came back? A horrible image invaded her mind without mercy. She shuddered at the thought of Tom snatching her sister while she wasn't around to protect her. With a pounding heart, she opened her mouth to refuse the little girl, but the pressure of Toni's hand on her arm stopped her.

Apparently sensing her hesitation, Katie looked at her with wide, soulful eyes.

She just didn't have the heart to say no. "I guess it'll be all right. If it's truly okay with Mrs. Kane."

Amanda nodded, her face softening with relief. "That sounds fine. Good-bye, Fannie. It was very nice to meet you. I-uh-hope to see you again soon. Let's go, girls."

"Thank you, Fannie!" Two giggling little girls dashed off through the prairie grass. "Nice to meet you, Becca," Fannie called after them.

The little girl stopped, turned, and waved. "You too,

ma'am." Then they both turned and resumed their jaunt. Fannie smiled after them.

"That's a nice sight to see," Toni said.

"I know. The twins desperately need to have a little fun."

"I agree. But I was talking about your smile. It's nice to see you in better spirits."

Fannie sobered as Toni's words reminded her of just why she had to keep her guard up. "I just can't help but worry about Tom and George coming back."

Toni dismissed her worry with a roll of her green eyes. "We have nothing to worry about. Between Blake and Sam Two Feathers, we're plenty safe."

One name was noticeably absent. "And Hank?"

It was pretty evident to all that Hank was sweet on Toni. But Toni kept him at arm's length. Fannie observed how she carefully avoided being alone with him. Even now, a troubled frown creased her brow. "You okay?" Fannie asked.

"I don't know. I keep remembering something, but I'm not sure I should mention it."

"About Hank?" Fannie felt the discomfort in her own chest.

Toni nodded and gathered a breath. "Do you remember anything about the day we left Hawkins?

"Of course. Every detail."

"I mean . . . anything in . . . particular." A troubled frown creased her brow, and Fannie had a sudden, sick feeling that Toni was about to voice the same fear she'd held in since that horrible day.

"Fannie"—Toni's eyes sought hers with a spark of fear

blinking out from beneath long eyelashes—"when Hank came out to say good-bye, did you notice something?"

A wave of nausea rolled through Fannie's stomach. There was no denying what Hank had done. Slowly, she nodded. "Blood smeared on the legs of his britches."

"Yes. As though he had wiped off a knife." She flicked the reins as the oxen slowed down, trying to snatch a few blades of prairie grass.

"He said he had him all tied up and was going to wait and take him back to town after we got away." Even though Fannie had considered the necessity of killing the man, she'd have never been able to go through with it. The thought that Hank had committed such an act, so cold-bloodedly, wiped off his knife, and swaggered out of the barn to say good-bye without so much as an ounce of remorse clouding his eyes, was almost unthinkable. "You think he might have killed Arnold?"

Toni looked at her askance. "If not, then where was Arnold the other night when George and Tom showed up? I've never known George to do his own dirty work. He must have been desperate. I'd lay odds on it, Fannie. Arnold's dead, and Hank's the one who killed him."

"You think that's why he came along on the trail?"

"Partly." Her voice remained stoic. "I'm the other reason."

"Did he ask you to marry him?"

"No. He's already married." Her nostrils flared slightly as her chest rose and fell in a deep breath. "Has a wife out on a little farm east of town. Didn't you know that?"

Fannie blinked in surprise. "No. I truly didn't. How come we never saw her?"

"Hank never wanted her in town. She stayed home with their four children. She's full-blooded Cheyenne Indian."

"You mean he just abandoned them?"

Toni's shoulders lifted in a shrug. "That's the way it looks."

"How's she going to survive?"

"Hank figures she'll go back to her people."

"Doesn't he even care about his children?"

A shrug lifted her shoulders. "Apparently not."

Fighting against anger and loyalty toward the same man, Fannie shook her head. "I just can't believe it. We couldn't have gotten free without him."

She nodded. "I know. He always had a soft spot for you three. Your mama was kind to him, and your pa gave him his first job when he came to town. He felt an obligation."

Fannie tried to wrap her mind around the implication that Hank had abandoned his wife and children and murdered a man so that he could follow Toni, a prostitute, out West.

She looked ahead, past the wagon in front of her, and saw Hank riding down the line checking on the wagons one by one as he and several other men did throughout the day. As if sensing her gaze, he glanced her way and waved.

"I just don't know what I'm going to do, Fannie."

"What do you mean?"

"I-I think he's not quite hinged in the head altogether. Do you know what I mean?"

"You mean you think he's crazy?"

"Not all the way. Just enough so that you can't predict what he might do if he gets angry enough. That's why I haven't had the gumption to tell him I'm not interested in continuing a relationship with him. Now or ever."

"Has he . . . ?"

Toni shook her head. "Not yet, but I recognize that look in his eyes. He'll be coming around soon and expecting something for his efforts. Something more than a kiss and a hug."

Cheeks burning, Fannie felt her throat close, and she swallowed back a cough. "Well, don't give it to him." She dreaded the very thought of what Blake would do if he found out Toni was so much as looking with favor on a man, let alone submitting to improper advances.

"I don't plan on it," Toni replied dryly. "But I don't know what he might do if I say no too many times. There are only so many excuses and only a certain length of time a man will be patient."

"Then what are you going to do?"

Again, she shrugged. "For now, I can hold him off. We can be thankful that he fancies himself in love with me. That'll buy me some time."

"How so?"

A grim smile touched her lips. "Men in love are more willing to wait for what they want from the woman they want. Men who only want one thing aren't. Hank expects us to live together in Oregon and lead our neighbors to believe we're husband and wife. All his dreams are swept up in us living a grand happily ever after."

"Shh, here he comes," Fannie said in a hushed tone. She smiled brightly. "Good afternoon, Hank."

The man flushed brightly around his bushy beard. "Goin'

perty good. Blake's callin' a halt up ahead, next to the Big Blue River. We'll be crossin' over in the mornin'."

Worry hit Fannie, clenching her gut. "Will the oxen be swimming across?"

He nodded. "Only a fool would pay the prices that ferry operator's askin' per wagon when the water's this calm, and it don't look like we're in for no rain."

"H-how much to ferry across?"

"Two dollars per wagon." Hank's eyes narrowed. "You ain't thinkin' of payin' it, are ya? Blake won't take kindly to it. Figures a person ought to stick to the plan. He's tellin' everyone to prepare to ford the river and not pay for the ferry."

Fannie's shoulders squared. Blake Tanner could force her to pick up buffalo chips, he could assign her a spot in the train, could force her to stay away from the single men of the train; but he couldn't tell her where to spend her own money. "We'll be taking the ferry," she said with a stubborn nod.

Hank's thick eyebrows shifted upward, then he gave a laugh. "Suit yerself, girlie. I reckon you've earned the right to do as ya please."

"Does that go for me too, Hank?" Toni asked, staying carefully guarded and smiling as though teasing.

Hank's eyes narrowed for a split second, then his face cracked into a grin. "Sure does, honey. As long as you please to stick with me." He tipped his ragged hat in an attempt at manners. "I gotta get along and let the rest of these folks know we'll be stopping soon. I'll be around for supper."

When he was out of earshot, Toni expelled a long, slow breath. The woman was right. Hank wasn't going to let her go, and, unless Fannie was mistaken, refusing him might be slightly more dangerous for Toni than George could ever be.

She gave an involuntary shudder. "Think we ought to talk to Blake about this?"

Toni shook her head. "No. Blake would figure I deserved whatever Hank has in mind. He won't lift a finger against a man who hasn't done anything wrong."

"Yet."

"Yeah . . ."

Blake faced the onslaught of blue sparking at him from Fannie's enormous eyes. He understood her fear of the crossing. The first time feeling the wagon wheels lose solid ground and being at the mercy of oxen who might or might not be able to pull together during the swim was disconcerting. Blake had seen his share of drownings, but usually those incidents were a result of carelessness either of the wagon master who had no business allowing a crossing of a rough, swollen river, or a driver who tried to rush across.

"As long as you take it slow and let the oxen know who's boss, you'll be fine," he said evenly, trying to reassure the young woman.

"I already forked over my two dollars to Mr. White for a ride across, and I aim to get my money's worth, Mr. Tanner," she said with stubborn resolve. "I'll meet you on the other side."

Tarnation, she was one difficult little woman. "Listen, Fannie. If I let you take the ferry, every woman feeling nervous about the crossing is going to force her man to pay money they can't afford to ferry across. It'll take us two days instead of half a day to get everyone over. We'll lose more time we can't afford to lose. The water is gentle, and there hasn't been rain in several days according to Mr. White."

Stubbornness wilted into consideration and he held his breath. She gave a slow nod. "All right, Blake. I can see your point. I'll do my best."

Surprise and admiration lifted in Blake's chest.

"I'll get my wagon out of the line with the special wagons as soon as I talk to Mr. White and get my money back."

Blake placed a restraining hand on her arm. He knew better. Louis White would never refund her money. He'd take a bullet first. "It'll save time if you get your wagon back in place in our line. I'll get your two dollars."

"He charged me three," she admitted with a sheepish blush of pink tingeing her cheeks, forcing her freckles to pop out in an attractive spray across her nose.

"Why'd he do that?"

"He said the extra people in our wagon would weigh down the ferry, and he had to charge more."

"And you paid it?" Only a greenhorn would fall for that kind of lie.

"What other choice did I have?"

"The same choice you have right now. Ford the river."

Anger shot to her eyes, and her mouth opened, ready to release an onslaught that Blake had neither time nor temperament to receive. He quickly covered her mouth with his hand. Her eyes widened with surprise. "Enough," he said. "I'll get your *three* dollars while you get yourself back in line."

Without a word, she yanked his hand from her mouth, swung around, and stomped back to the wagon.

The memory of her soft, warm breath on his palm burned through Blake as he reached into his pocket, removed three bills, and prepared to hand them over to the bullheaded beauty. No sense in going through the motions of talking things over with Mr. White. As much as he hated the idea of parting with even two bits of the money he had saved to purchase supplies once he arrived in Oregon, he couldn't take a chance on the grim scenario he'd painted for Fannie. They had lost too much time already between Hawkins and Fannie's injuries. His heart stirred with unrest. The journey wasn't a month old. There were at least five more to go, and already they'd been overburdened with problems. He could only hope . . . pray, even . . . that it would be smooth going from here on out.

At the first odd feeling of the wagon swaying in the water as the bulky oxen made way through the rippling water of the Big Blue River, Fannie tightened with panic. She'd never learned to swim and neither had the twins. Her overactive imagination couldn't shake the very real possibility that she might end up bobbing up and down in the water gasping, crying, begging for help, only to drown seconds before rescue came. That Blake Tanner. She just flat couldn't bear the sight of him.

Resentment overtook panic at the thought of Blake's smug face when he handed back her three dollars from Mr. White. "Tuck this away and stop spending your money so recklessly if you intend to make a decent life out West for yourselves."

Then he'd ridden away without giving her a chance to tell him to mind his own business and that she and the twins would make out just fine, thank you very much.

She was so worried about the water in general that she hadn't even taken much time to worry about the fact that they were crossing into Pawnee country, according to Blake. His assurance that the Indians only wanted to trade and occasionally stole a bit of livestock didn't make her feel any better. She'd banished the twins to the back of the wagon amid wild protests. But she sat firm on her bench next to Toni, who thankfully seemed calm and competent.

"You're doing well, Miss Toni," called Sam Two Feathers from the right side of the wagon.

Toni kept a firm grip on the reins and concentrated on the oxen. Her simple nod at the praise didn't seem to offend Sam at all. Sam looked past her to Fannie. "It won't be long, now, Miss Caldwell. Keep your eyes on the far bank, and you'll be there before you know it."

"Thanks, Sam," Fannie replied miserably. He gave her a smile and waved, then swam his horse back to the other shore to allow the next wagon to start across. Only two were allowed in the water at a time, but Willard James and his brood had just made it to shore ahead of them. Fannie envied the family and could not help but wish she'd been in their spot. Then they'd already be out of the water and on dry ground once more.

Besides, her ribs ached with bruised tightness, and the motion of the wagon induced mild nausea that she feared would venture into full-blown vomiting before long.

"We're halfway there," Toni said through stiff lips, as though reassuring herself as much as Fannie.

"You're doing good. Like Sam said."

"The oxen are getting tired. They're slowing down."

Fannie's heart picked up, but she refused to give in to the rush of fear. Now was the time to be strong for Toni's sake. "They just have to work harder, that's all. Don't worry. We're almost there."

Toni nodded, but the tension in her face didn't relax.

The oxen seemed to struggle less as they saw that their destination was within reach. They drew within a few yards of the bank, and Fannie began to relax. Just as it appeared all would be well, a scream and a splash split the air. "Kip!" came Katie's wail. "Fannie! Help!" Fannie whipped around, half-hanging off the side of the wagon and saw Kip flailing in the water. She saw Blake and Sam headed toward Kip on horseback, but they were so far away they might as well have been in Hawkins. Fannie couldn't imagine them getting to the boy in time. Without thought to the reality that she couldn't even swim, Fannie stood. "I'm coming, Kip. Hang on." Suddenly her feet left solid ground, and she was immersed in water, fighting a force to be reckoned with: her own inability to save her brother.

Nine

Two fierce emotions shocked through Blake within seconds of one another. First, relief, when Fannie stood in the wagon and he realized she was going after the boy. But in the seconds after she hit the water, another emotion stabbed at his gut: cold fear as he realized by her splashing about that the young woman had no idea how to swim any more than her brother.

She disappeared under the water, then reappeared, reaching one slender hand in desperation. His heart nearly stopped at the sight. "Help!" she gulped, before sliding underwater once more.

"Sam!" he called, sliding off Dusty and swimming furiously toward Fannie's panicked form.

"I'll get the boy," he heard Sam call.

There was no time to watch and make sure the scout reached Kip. Fannie dipped below the water's surface once more. She didn't have much time before the river claimed her for its own.

Fannie hadn't prayed in ages, but she prayed now. *Don't let Kip die.* She felt herself sinking for what seemed like the hundredth time. Death didn't scare her. Except that she didn't want to leave the twins alone. She'd tried. She hoped they would know that she'd tried to save Kip, and she'd struggled to keep herself afloat. But it was no use. She knew she was drowning in the black, still water. Funny, it hadn't seemed black before. It was green and blue and lovely if not fearsome. But now everything seemed black and cold and still . . .

"Fannie! Wake up. Fannie!" Her cheeks stung as a heavy hand slapped at her. Then pounded her back. Her chest screamed as though it would burst any second, and she coughed and coughed.

"That's it," someone called from far, far away. "Let the river come out of you."

The river? What was it doing in her? Oh, now she remembered. She'd drowned. "Am I dead?" she whispered.

"What was that?"

She recognized Blake's voice but was still unable to connect with reality. "Did I get you killed too?"

"Not quite." His voice sounded gruff, and Fannie inwardly cringed. She hoped this wouldn't be the last straw before he tossed her out on her backside. "Why'd you jump in if you didn't know how to swim?" he demanded, as she opened her eyes and focused on the brightly lit world around her. No, she wasn't dead. Hell would be hot and fiery, Heaven would be bright like this, but as hateful as he was, Blake probably wouldn't be there. The thought gave her a second of grim satisfaction. Then she realized she hadn't answered his question.

"Kip was drowning." With a gasp, she sat up, the blood rushing to her head and blinding her with a wave of dizziness. "Where's Kip?" She squeezed her eyes shut, trying to ward off the light-headedness.

"I'm here, Fannie."

"Oh, thank God." And she truly meant that. She'd prayed, and God had answered. When was the last time that had happened?

"Lie down before you fall and hit your head on a rock." Blake forced her back, surprisingly gentle, considering his tone. "How did you expect to save him when you couldn't swim either? Are you weak in the head?" His voice bespoke frustration, and again Fannie's stomach tightened with worry and a bit of her own frustration at the mounting insults.

"I didn't know. I didn't really think about it, Blake."

"Well, maybe you should start thinking," he snapped. "Instead of saving one person, we ended up having to save both of you. Barely." He gave her a sharp look, allowing the last word to take effect before continuing. "Then where would Katie be? Alone, that's where."

Fannie's strength was beginning to return, along with a surge of anger. "You've made your point."

"I hope so. Because if you cause one more delay . . ."

He left the sentence for Fannie to finish on her own and shoved to his feet. "Sadie, please look after her until she's strong enough to walk back to her wagon. Kip, run and let Toni know Fannie's going to be along later, then get started unhitching the oxen and turn them out for the night. We'll push on in the morning."

Fannie refused to watch him leave. Refused to cry the bitter, angry tears that threatened just below the surface. And refused to give him the satisfaction of lying around camp all night nursing her aching body. She sat up. "I'll get to my chores."

Sadie's sudden burst of laughter shook Fannie to the core. "What's so funny?" she demanded.

"You're not going nowhere, missy. Just lie back down on those hides and rest like Blake said, and I'll bring you some strong, hot coffee."

"I'm perfectly able to pick up buffalo chips."

"Honey"—Sadie's voice grew gentle—"I admire your gumption. But you've been through some pretty harsh ordeals lately. The best thing you can do for yourself and everyone else is to heal up and stop causing trouble."

"I don't mean to cause trouble," she mumbled, feeling the reprimand all the way to her toes.

"I know that," Sadie said, bringing a tin mug filled with rich-smelling brew and handing it to Fannie. Without asking, she helped Fannie sit up and settled her against a tall birch tree. "And in his heart of hearts, Blake knows it too. But this is his last train west. He didn't bank on someone like you comin' in and upsetting things. He's pretty set in his ways, in case you hadn't noticed."

Fannie gave a wry grin. "Only a blind, deaf dog wouldn't notice." As much as she hated to initiate any conversation that involved Blake, her curiosity got the better of her. "How come this is his last train?" She took a sip of the scalding coffee, trying to pretend she was only mildly interested.

"It's time for him to settle down and start thinking about his future." The older woman gave her a look that made Fannie avert her gaze to the mug in her hands. "I suspect he's looking for a wife."

Fannie gave a snort. "With his personality, he'd have better luck finding gold in Hawkins."

"Don't sell him too short. Blake's a good man. You should think about it."

Fannie's throat tightened, and she swallowed her bite with difficulty. "You're suggesting I marry Blake?"

"Well, it wouldn't hurt to set your cap for him. You could do worse." She settled down with her own steaming mug. "So could he."

Had the woman lost her mind? "Miss Sadie, Blake hates me. He really does. First he didn't want me coming on the train since I don't have a man to take care of me. Then I forced him into it by showing up and threatening to follow along anyway. And I've caused him no end of trouble. If you're suggesting he would think twice about me, you're sorely mistaken."

Sadie gave a smug smile. "I'm rarely mistaken about these things, my dear."

"Well, you are this time."

They fell into silence. Fannie took a few more sips of the coffee, then set her mug aside. "I best get back to our wagon and check on Toni and the twins."

"Here, let me help you."

"Thank you," Fannie said as she was hauled to her feet, more than helped.

"You're most welcome." Sadie gave her a quick hug and turned her loose just as fast. "Before you go, I have a little gift for you."

"A gift?" Suspicion caused her to shrink back. She didn't accept gifts, especially not from someone she didn't even know. She'd had learned all too well that gifts usually demanded a hefty price. And she was through paying.

But Sadie was already walking the few steps toward her own wagon. "Wait there."

"No, Mrs. Barnes, I couldn't accept anything."

"Nonsense. Don't be so suspicious."

Too stunned to move, Fannie remained where she stood until Sadie emerged seconds later and climbed down with something in her hand. She held out a beautiful pair of gloves. Fannie eyed the offering in wonder but didn't reach for them. "Why are you giving these to me?"

"I made them for you." Sadie pressed the gloves into Fannie's hand, and she had no choice but to wrap her hands around the soft leather.

"I don't understand."

"Fine if you're going to drag it out of me. Blake brought the deerskin a few days ago and asked me to make it into a pair of gloves for you so that your hands won't blister and bleed once you start driving the team again."

Blinking, Fannie tried to wrap her mind around this startling revelation. "Blake?"

"That's right. And I happen to know he was saving that hide until he got a couple more, and I was going to make him a new buckskin shirt." She gave Fannie another smug grin. "So you see . . . like I said before, you could do worse."

"But . . . why would he do that? He doesn't even know me, let alone fancy me that way."

"Blake's got a heart as big as the West itself. The sight of your bloody hands likely did him in."

"I've never thought of him as having that big a heart." As a matter of fact, from where she sat most of the time, she wasn't sure he possessed a heart at all.

"Well, you haven't known him long, Missy."

"I don't stick around to get to know a skunk when I see one either, but that doesn't mean I can't figure out that I don't want anything to do with it."

A chuckle shook the woman's shoulders. "Well, you got a point there. Nonetheless"—she nodded toward the gloves still clutched in Fannie's hands—"would a skunk give up his hide for you?"

Fannie walked carefully past the woman on her way back to her own wagon. "I wouldn't want him to."

"You're one stubborn young woman."

"My ma used to say that about me." The pain of living a sweet memory pricked at Fannie. Usually, she pushed the memories aside at the first sting, but tonight, she pressed on. "Pa used to tell her, 'Not stubborn, darlin'. Just determined. That attitude will get her far in life.'"

"And has it?"

Raising her chin against the very thought that this woman might be implying her pa was wrong about anything let alone his prophecy about her future, she sniffed. "Not yet, but that's why I'm headed west. There's no telling how far I might go."

"That's true, Missy. You're going as far as the trail leads. And when you get there, it's up to you whether or not you carve out a good life for yourself or whether you fail and end up worse off than when you left."

"I can't imagine anything could be worse than slaving away for Tom."

A far-off look softened Sadie's eyes. "There are worse things."

Instinctively, Fannie knew not to pry, so she allowed the woman her private memories. "Good night, Miss Sadie," she said pressing the woman's work-roughened hand. "Thank you for taking care of me and for the gloves."

"You're welcome." The woman seemed to snap out of her melancholy and turned with a smile. "Now you remember what I said . . . you could do worse than setting your cap for Blake Tanner. He would gladly take care of the woman that captures his heart."

"I don't need a man to take care of me."

"Unless you jump in the river."

Swift heat rushed to Fannie's cheeks, but she wasn't about to argue with a woman her mother's age. "Good night, ma'am."

Walking toward her wagon, she couldn't help but replay Sadie's words. "He would gladly take care of the woman who captures his heart." Fannie's response to Sadie had been true. She didn't need or want anyone taking care of her. But she couldn't help but thrill to one thought: What would it be like to capture the heart of a man like Blake?

Ten

The setting sun cast a glorious red glow over the still waters of the Big Blue River. Blake breathed in a grateful burst of fresh, cool air as his mind replayed the image of Fannie and Kip struggling for air—for life itself—this afternoon. Conflicting emotions warred within his breast. On one hand he wished he'd stuck to his guns and never allowed the strong-willed woman to join the train. On the other hand, he couldn't stop thinking about the fiery red curls clinging to her face and neck as she stared at him with stormy eyes insisting she had no choice but to try and save her brother, no matter the risk to her own life. Admiration warred with aggravation. Attraction with frustration. He tried to push her out of his mind as he mounted Dusty and began his nightly ride through the wagon train to assure himself all was well.

"Good evening, Mr. Tanner," came a sweet voice as he passed the Cooper wagon. A rush of heat hit Blake's neck as he spotted Edna Cooper. Looking closer, he noted she was alone, so he waved, replied to her greeting in kind, and continued his ride through the camp without pausing for conversation. He saw her face cloud with disappointment as he passed, and regret shifted through him. He hated to make any woman feel slighted. The girl was uncommonly pretty. Submissive and gentle. A good cook and a good mother. Everything Blake was looking for. He had shown her plenty of attention the first couple of weeks of their journey. But the last couple of weeks . . . well, Fannie had come into his life, and since then, as much as he hated to admit the truth, he couldn't think of anyone but her. Of course, Fannie would be the last person he'd be likely to marry. She wore trousers for one thing. Tried to be too independent and manly. Although she did look sort of nice in the britches. But they put ideas into a man's head that ought not be there. And, he'd noticed how they made the other women in the wagon train uncomfortable.

Sam joined him on his mare. "Mrs. Cooper doesn't look happy that you didn't stop and speak with her."

Blake shrugged. "No time tonight. I'm sure she understands."

"Women typically don't understand when a man stops showing interest for no apparent reason."

"I have a reason." Blake winced and wished he could draw the impulsive words back.

"Miss Fannie."

It wasn't a question, more like an observation. Humiliated that he'd been so transparent of late, Blake figured he should take this time to set his friend straight. "Yes, Fannie. Since she joined us, I've been busy getting her out of one mess or another until I'm too distracted even to think about courting another woman."

There, he'd said enough of the truth to pull Sam's thoughts away from any romantic connection between Blake and Fannie.

"I see," Sam said.

"Fannie's a heap of trouble. I'm thinking of dropping off the whole group, including Toni, at the next hole of a town we come to."

"According to my scouts, that'll be in about a week."

"Are we off course? To my recollection there's not a town or a fort for the next hundred miles."

Sam gave a shrug. "Must have started up since last year. Maybe folks who didn't want to keep going to Oregon just stopped and built their own town. They got a saloon, a general store, even got themselves a sheriff and a church."

It sounded like a dozen more prairie towns just like it. That's the way it had been since he signed on with his first wagon train ten years ago going back and forth across the country. Towns sprang up overnight and many died just as quickly. Some, like St. Louis, grew fast and kept growing. Others didn't have a chance.

"Should I tell Miss Fannie to prepare to leave us at the next town?"

Sam's words startled Blake from his musings, and he couldn't gather his wits quick enough to pretend indifference. "Of course not," he growled. Without another word, he nudged Dusty forward, leaving the chuckling scout behind to form his own opinion.

Wistful puffs of smoke rose from campfires throughout the circle of a hundred wagons. Oxen and horses were hobbled and set out within the enormous circle to graze upon the prairie grass. Blake could hear the soft laughter of children playing, banging of pots and pans as women prepared their evening meals. He stopped at Sadie's wagon and looked around, staring at the spot next to the fire where he'd carried Fannie, still feeling her wet, shivering body in his arms.

"She's gone," Sadie said, nodding toward the empty hides.

"Where?" Hang it all. Was there anyone who didn't read his growing feelings for that confounded woman?

"Back to her own wagon."

"I thought I told you to take care of her." He heard the gruffness of his tone and knew Sadie wasn't going to take it quietly. Bracing himself for the tongue-lashing he knew he had coming, he formed his apology in his mind.

"What was I supposed to do, tie her to a tree?" Sadie's eyebrows scrunched together in a fierce frown. "Besides, I'm not her nursemaid. She's a grown woman with more spunk than any woman ought to have, and she makes up her own mind."

"You're right," Blake replied humbly. "I'm sorry I accused you. That woman is driving me to distraction." How was he supposed to take care of her if she kept ignoring his orders?

Her brow shot up in surprise and her face softened with amusement. "Oh, honey. Hop down off that horse and have some of these beans and corn bread. I know it's the same fare as the last two nights. But there's going to be a treat tomorrow. A couple of the hunters brought in some venison, and we'll be having a campwide roast tomorrow after we make camp."

Willing to accept her quick forgiveness, Blake slid from his horse and took the proffered tin plate of filling, well-cooked food. He walked to an empty pickle barrel next to the fire and took his first bite before he was all the way seated. "Thanks," he said around a bite of corn bread.

"Have you eaten anything today?" she asked, hands on her hips, lips scrunched in a maternal scowl.

He shook his head, suddenly feeling guilty beneath her scolding. "No time. What with the river crossing and all."

"Mrs. Cooper must have forgotten you and Sam at breakfast today." Her eyes were completely guileless, but Blake knew better.

"I thanked her for her generosity and told her we couldn't keep accepting breakfast from her."

"Oh? Think she got the message?"

"What message?"

"The one where you're trying to back away from what was starting to be a courtship?"

"The only thing going on between us is breakfast, and I put a stop to that."

"Well, that's fine as long as you don't forget to eat something on your own."

"I do just fine. I don't need a woman telling me to eat."

"Hrmph. You'll be taking time to pick yourself up off the ground if you don't take better care of yourself on these busy days. How do you plan to keep your strength if you don't eat?"

This must be what it was like to have a real mother, Blake thought, and not for the first time either when confronted with Miss Sadie's tendency to boss him around. His own mother took grudging care of him between the hours of one in the afternoon, when she finally hauled herself out of bed hungover, face paint smeared across her face, and five o'clock, when her customers began arriving to take up thirty minutes of her time. For a couple of years, there had been one nice black woman who worked in the kitchen and cleaned the saloon and hotel. She had petted him and saved him special treats from the kitchen. But the owner of the saloon had lost her to one of the miners in a poker game, and that was the end of Blake's experience with maternal care.

That is, until Sadie stopped him months ago, determined to join the train.

He'd told her the same thing he told every other single woman who wanted to go west, but Sadie had pretended not to hear him and showed up in Independence, Missouri anyway, bright and early, fully loaded, and ready to go.

For some reason that he still couldn't fathom, he'd assigned her a spot ten wagons down the line, without a word. She'd taken him under her wing like a mama hen that first day, and he'd been there ever since.

"So, uh, how was Fannie? Did she do okay after I left?"

"Oh, sure. Feisty as ever, that one."

"Angry at me, I presume?"

The woman gave him a twinkle-eyed smile. "Called you a

skunk and said she didn't want to hang around waiting to get sprayed. Or something to that effect."

A funny, sort of disappointed surprise hit him square in the gut. "I wonder why she'd say a thing like that."

"Pride mostly."

"Pride?"

"Yep. She's as stubborn and full of pride as you are. You're both smitten but neither will admit it."

"Smitten?" Blake gave a frown. "You've been in the sun too much today. The woman is impossible, and I'm strongly considering unloading her whole wagonful at the next town. Which Sam informed me is only two days away."

"Sure you are," she said, with more than a little humor tingeing her voice.

"You don't believe me?" he asked with determination. Maybe he should just show Sam and Sadie that he wasn't going to turn into a jar of apple preserves over this woman. Rules were rules, and she'd caused more than her share of trouble.

Sadie took his plate and walked over to the fire to dip him another spoonful. "Simmer down before you go off half-cocked and do something you'll regret just to prove a point." She shoved the plate back into his hands.

"I don't have anything to prove." He forked a chunk of bean-covered ham. "I'm leading this train. What I say goes."

Wisely, Sadie clamped her lips together. Blake breathed easier, knowing that settled it. He ate, but each bite was harder to swallow as he began to get the uncomfortable feeling her silence wasn't exactly acquiescence.

"Don't you think she ought to be tossed out on her ear?"

"That's not my call, hon." She took his empty plate and handed him a cup of coffee.

"Thanks," he said, taking the tin mug. "But if it were your call?"

She took her own coffee and settled down across from him on a turned-over washtub. "Blake, this young woman has been through an awful lot in her short life."

"She told you that? More than just a few beatings here and there." Blake perked up. He had his suspicions about what she'd been through, especially after seeing how the bloated old storekeeper looked at her. The very memory brought his blood to a quick boil.

"She doesn't have to tell me. A woman knows."

Well, there was no arguing against women's intuition. And he wasn't fool enough to try. "So just because she's been through a lot, I should overlook her ignorant actions."

"You mean like jumping in after her brother when she saw how far away you were from the middle of the river?"

Well, yeah, something like that. But Blake could see her point and decided to be more reasonable than his building anger would normally allow.

"She has to stop disrupting this wagon train," he said, giving voice to his frustration. "I can't think straight for worry what she's going to get into next."

"Listen, Blake. I know it seems like she's brought you no end of trouble."

"Seems like?"

"What has she done really?"

"Followed after the train when I told her she wasn't welcome."

"Which is exactly what I would have done if you hadn't graciously allowed me a spot."

Blake felt a blush creep up his neck and singe his cheeks. "Well, that's different. You didn't bring a pair of ornery twins and a saloon girl with you."

"That's true." Her lips twitched, and Blake had the maddening feeling he was being mocked. "And I didn't get myself followed by a man who is nothing more than a slave trader if you ask me."

"Exactly." Wait. Whose point was she making?

Her plump shoulders rose and fell in a wistful sigh. "There's not one person on this earth who cares whether I live or die. Certainly no one who cares whether I leave for the West or not. So I'm easy to put up with."

Blake wanted to reach out to the woman whose voice had suddenly grown soft with pain. He wanted to tell her that he cared whether she lived or died. That he was glad she had come along on the trek and that he hoped they'd be neighbors for the rest of her life once they reached their destination, but that wasn't his way. Pretty words stuck in his throat, and his tongue refused to allow them voice. Instead, he stared at his cup and cleared his throat uncomfortably.

"Blake," she said. "Look at me."

He did.

"Fannie can't help it that she came to us wounded, then made it worse by refusing to let it show that first day. She can't help it that she was sold to that Tom fellow or that he didn't keep his end of the bargain and let her go a year ago when he was supposed to."

"I can't help it either," he muttered, trying not to envision everything she'd just said.

"No. You can't. But God has given you a unique opportunity to be His hands extended to her in grace."

"Grace? You mean just let her stay and disrupt this train because she's had a hard life? She's not the only person in this world who's had some tough breaks."

Sadie gave him a sad smile. "You're right. But she seems to be the one who needs the most help right now. And you seem to be the person who can help her. Remember, grace means that we receive God's goodness even though we don't deserve it."

"It does?"

"Um-hmm," she said sipping her coffee. She swallowed. "So, maybe in your eyes she deserves to be tossed aside. Maybe it would be easier for you if she's not around distracting you with those pretty blue eyes and curly red hair and feisty ways."

"That's not . . ."

She silenced him with upraised hands. "Let's not argue about it. My point is that you are the only one in a position to grant her grace. It's your choice." She stood, turned the washbasin over, and reached for a bucket of water.

Blake was on his feet in a flash. "Here, I'll get that for you."

Tenderness washed over her face. "Thank you, son."

Blake fought back a rush of affection and an overwhelming sense of longing for a mother who truly called him son. He had no right to feel this way about a woman who wasn't his ma. And who knew if she'd be around once they reached Oregon. She might end up two hundred miles away. She could die before they reached the promised land.

"You're welcome, Miz Barnes."

"I'll let you get back to your rounds."

Blake walked toward Dusty. "Thank you for supper. It was tasty."

"Come tomorrow, and I'll fix you some roast venison."

"Yes, ma'am," he said with practiced indifference. "We'll see."

"Well, good night."

Blake rode away, feeling lower than a worm squirming deep under the earth.

Fannie felt, rather than saw Blake coming on horseback. Dread shot through her. "Here he comes," Toni said softly. "Now you can thank him for those beautiful gloves."

"He didn't make them," she snapped.

"Fannie, don't be difficult."

She knew she was being cantankerous. But the very thought that Blake might think she'd set her cap for him made her feel downright mean. She'd had enough of men. She knew what they wanted behind closed doors.

"Honestly, Toni, I don't see how you can even want to go west and get married," she'd said to her friend one day.

"I've never experienced love," she'd replied with a dreamy

smile. "I just want to know what it feels like to be in the arms of a man I love."

"How can you say that? I know what goes on upstairs at the Gold Nugget."

Toni had turned to her and looked her square in the eye. "That has nothing to do with love. Love is when a man treats you real good. When you would follow him to the ends of the earth just for one look at his dirty face. When you delight in sewing his ripped trousers and cooking his favorite dinner."

Fannie had given a snort, unimpressed. "Sounds pretty one-sided to me."

Undaunted, Toni's head shook from side to side. "No, every time he carries in firewood or reaches for something high on a shelf for you, or opens a can of preserves. That's the way a man shows love. When he fixes the roof or carries up a ham from the smokehouse."

Fannie pushed aside the memory and the longing that conversation had produced in her.

"Hello, Mr. Blake," Toni called. "Would you care to stay for supper? Kip caught a couple of nice-sized catfish. I'm just getting ready to start frying them."

"No thanks," he said abruptly. "I ate with Sadie."

Toni's face fell. Fannie turned on Blake. "Can't you be even a little pleasant?"

"Apparently not pleasant enough for you," he retorted.

"You don't always have to be so mean to her. She isn't asking for anything. I don't even know why she bothers being nice to you the way you treat her."

"It's all right. Both of you." Toni gave her a little shove

forward. "Fannie was just saying that she needs to thank you for the beautiful gloves."

Now why did she have to go and tell a lie like that? Fannie fumed, but knew she had no choice now. She cleared her throat. "They're fine."

Blake's eyes narrowed, but Toni jumped in again. "Now, Fannie. Tell Mr. Tanner what you said earlier."

Blinking, Fannie tried to search her mind for the comment Toni was referring to. Suddenly, Toni gave a laugh that Fannie didn't believe and waved her hand nonchalantly. "She's just too shy to say so, but Fannie told me these were the softest gloves she's ever seen, and they feel just like second skin on her hands."

Oh. Well, she hadn't said it exactly like that. But she supposed it was close enough to what she meant. But why did Toni have to go and get such a big mouth all of a sudden? Fannie wouldn't have said that much. She'd thanked him, and that was enough. Men never did anything without a price, and she wasn't going to give Blake so much as a smile, let alone anything else as payment.

"Don't worry, Mr. Tanner. I won't slow down the train anymore. Those gloves will do just the trick and keep me working."

Blake stared speechless. He frowned in confusion, then his expression turned to anger. "Let's hope so, because we can't abide any more delays."

Alarm squeezed Fannie nearly in two. Her bravado left her, and she met Blake's gaze earnestly. "You have my word. Please excuse me." She swung around and stalked back to the wagon before he could note the fear in her eyes or the quake in her voice. She climbed inside and sat against the side, knees pressed up to her chest. Sitting in the stuffy solitude, she made a decision. No longer would Blake Tanner have cause to regret their presence in his precious wagon train. From now on, she was going to pull her weight and then some. No matter what, Blake wasn't going to have any excuse to turn her and her little band out on the open prairie.

Eleven

Blake knew better than to let down his guard. Still, after two weeks without incident, he was starting to relax and ease back into the familiar life on the trail. True to her word, Fannie had become a model member of the wagon train. She did her share of the work and then some. Had learned to hitch and unhitch the oxen without help. He had to admit, he enjoyed watching her wearing those gloves more than he ever thought he would. Knowing her hands weren't shredded and bleeding made the sacrifice more than worth it.

A request had been made to stop early on Saturday night and get the wagon train ready for a wedding between one of Willard James's girls and Harvey Luther's son, Thomas. Passing a town with a preacher had been more than Thomas had been willing to let go. He was ready to marry the girl of his choice.

Since he was in such a good mood, and since the weather had been so cooperative lately, helping them make up for lost time, Blake had decided to allow it. Since the announcement, three more couples had come forward with their intention to marry that night.

So now at noon on a perfect day to stay on the trail, he had called a halt beside a creek. After chores, the ladies had ordered the men to stay away from the water while they took time to bathe and try to look presentable for the night's festivities.

He had to admit, the charge of excitement in the air was becoming infectious, and he thought he might cast off his buckskins and don a pair of trousers and a white shirt for the occasion. Come to think of it, a dip in the creek would probably do him some good, and maybe he could talk Sadie into taking her shears to his nearly shoulder-length hair.

And perhaps he'd take a turn around the dance floor with two or three of the women of the train. He was due for a little fun. The thought lifted his spirits even more, and he headed away from his own campfire in search of Sadie.

Sam rode into camp and made a beeline for Blake. By the serious look on his friend's face, Blake knew his two weeks of no trouble were over.

Fannie entered her wagon, feeling fresh and clean and wonderful after a dip in the creek. She sat on the wagon floor brushing her hair and staring at the trousers she'd been wearing for weeks. Part of her longed to cast off the manly clothes and don more appropriate attire, but since she'd carelessly thought of only enough material for Katie to have a couple of new dresses, she had only herself to blame.

Fannie couldn't help but catch the excitement traveling

through camp at the reality of a wedding and a dance, and, of course, Toni was downright swooning at the thought. The twins were beside themselves and were barely manageable even upon threat of being sent to bed early and not being allowed to join the celebration. But they knew she was only bluffing and paid her no mind.

She smiled at the memory and was just twisting her hair back into a knot at the nape of her neck when a soft tap on the wagon drew her attention. She crawled to the wagon and lifted aside the flap.

"Mrs. Cooper." In four weeks, this was the first time the woman had made any sort of overture toward her, so the words came from her mouth with a lilt of surprise.

Edna Cooper's cheeks tinged pink. "You're probably wondering why I'm here."

"A little, yes." There was no point in lying about it.

"I just hoped I could speak with you."

"Certainly. I'll be out in just a minute." She set the brush down, patted her damp hair, and tied the flap out of the way.

The other woman stepped back so Fannie could climb from the wagon. From a distance, Edna Cooper had not appeared so tall. But Fannie had to look up to meet her eyes. She was a lovely woman. Jealousy pinched her at the thought of this woman bringing breakfast to Blake. She noticed the woman carried a garment over her arm. "What can I do for you, Mrs. Cooper?"

A slow smile touched her perfectly curved mouth. "Please call me Edna. Mrs. Cooper makes me feel old, and I'd bet

I'm not more than two years older than you are."

"All right, Edna." Fannie couldn't help but return the smile.

Edna pushed the garment toward her. "I brought you this."

Fannie stared at the lovely blue gown of silk and lace. Then stared back up at the young widow. "I don't understand." Did she seem like a charity case that everyone suddenly wanted to give her gifts?

"Please don't be offended." Her soft voice pleaded with sincerity, and Fannie felt herself relax.

"I've been working on this since they announced we'd be stopping for a wedding and celebration."

Working on it?

"Oh, don't get me wrong. I didn't make it in three days." She laughed. "Heavens. What I meant was that I thought you might like a dress to wear to the wedding. I had so many that aren't suitable for the trail. I thought I'd never have a chance to wear them again. And I may not after tonight."

"Then you should wear it."

"It doesn't fit me anymore. That's what I meant when I said I've been working on it all week. Of course I could only guess at the right size, but I shortened it and took it in here and there. I'd be honored if you'd accept this as my welcome into the wagon train."

"I've been two wagons behind you for almost a month . . ."

Edna nodded, shamefaced. "This is a long-overdue gesture of friendship. I hope you'll accept it."

"I don't know . . ." Fannie eyed the beautiful gown. She'd

never owned anything so beautiful. In spite of herself, she reached out and fingered the silky material.

"Take it, Fannie. This blue was made to wear with eyes like yours. Blake won't be able to take his eyes off of you."

Fannie jerked her hand away as though the dress had suddenly risen to one hundred degrees. "Thank you just the same, Mrs. Cooper, but I can't accept. Please excuse me while I go to the Kanes' wagon and check on Katie."

Puzzlement clouded Edna's eyes. "I'm sorry if I've done or said anything wrong."

"No. You haven't. I like wearing britches, that's all. Dresses make me . . ." Fannie searched for a word. Any word. "Itch."

Blake strode toward Fannie's wagon, dreading the forthcoming conversation, but knowing it had to be done just the same. He almost ran into Edna walking toward him. He reached out to steady her. "Blake, I was coming to find you," she said breathlessly, touching her long, slender fingers to her collar.

"Can it wait? I need to speak with Miss Caldwell."

"She's not there." Edna's gaze focused down the line of wagons. "She said she was going to see about Katie."

"Tarnation." Blake shot a glance at the young widow. "Beg pardon."

"It's all right, Blake. Why don't you come to my campfire and have some coffee while we talk for a few minutes?"

What other choice did he have short of rudeness? Blake felt his own collar grow tighter as he followed Edna, dreading the scene sure to play out as soon as he had a cup of the hot bitter brew in his hands.

He sat on the tongue of her wagon and waited for the onslaught.

"Lovely day for a wedding," he said. Now, why'd he have to go and say a thing like that? he berated himself. She was sure enough going to think he was gearing up for a proposal.

Edna chuckled. "Oh, Blake. Don't look so afraid. I'm not going to beg for your love. And I'm certainly not waiting for you to ask for my hand in marriage."

Relieved, Blake took the cup she extended. "Is everything okay?"

She nodded. "I-I just wanted you to know that I've accepted Jason Stewart's proposal of marriage. We'll be getting married tonight with the rest."

Blake opened his mouth, and nothing came out. Absolutely no words entered his mind in response so he stared dumbly and waited for her to say something else.

"Jason is a good, kind man and will make a fine husband."

Blake nodded, finding his tongue. "Sure. He's a real good man. A woman could do worse than to marry up with Jason."

A rueful smile touched her lips. "I'm glad you approve."

Blake gave her a sheepish shrug. "Well, I do."

"I just wanted you to know I don't harbor any resentment toward you over your seeming change of affection."

Heat crawled up his neck and blasted his face. "I don't know what to say."

"You don't have to say anything, Blake. Fannie is a lovely girl."

Blake fought to keep from spitting out the sip of coffee. "Fannie? What are you talking about?"

"You might not be ready to admit it, but it's pretty obvious you're sweet on her."

He stood abruptly. "You're mistaken. My interest in Fannie is strictly the need to stay on my guard against whatever trouble she's going to cause next."

A knowing grin swept her face. "Have it your way. I'll see you later at the wedding."

"If I go."

Willard James grinned as soon as he stepped into the saloon. He'd suspected a town as soon as he'd seen that half-breed ride back into camp with a paper of some sort in his hands. And in these parts, wherever there was a town with paper, there was likely a saloon. Nearly a month had gone by since he'd wet his whistle with a bottle of whiskey, and he wasn't going to let Blake Tanner or anyone else tell him he couldn't do it.

He stepped up to the bar and ordered a whole bottle, and then swept the whiskey and a glass from the counter and found his way to a table where a game of cards was already in session.

"Hey, stranger," jawed an old-timer, his beard and hair snowy white, his hands shaking with age as he held his cards. "Want us to deal ya in?"

"Sure." Willard flashed his grin. The one that usually got him anything he wanted. A lazy-smiled cowpoke looked up from his hand and kicked out the chair across from him. "Have a seat."

"Don't mind if I do." Willard took the chair and sat. He poured himself a drink while he waited for the hand to end.

When all was said and done, three other men sat silently, morosely even, staring at the lazy-smiled cowpoke with resentment as he two-handedly raked his winnings from the center of the table and scooped them into his hat. He stretched back, lit a cigar, and stared at Willard. "You from the wagon train camped a few miles east of town?"

"We'll just keep that between us." After two shots of whiskey, he was beginning to feel amicable. "Let's deal the cards."

"Just a minute. Do these two look familiar?" He reached into his pocket and pulled out a document. Slowly, he unfolded the paper and slid it across the table. Willard eyed the wanted poster, lifted his gaze back to the man, and lied.

Toni was holding the blue gown when Fannie got back to the campsite with Katie in tow. "Look at this, Fannie. Someone left it here for you."

"How do you know it's for me?"

"Because it's too small for me and too big for Katie." Toni peered closer. "You already knew about this. Who did it?"

"Oh, Fannie," Katie breathed, reaching out gingerly to test the fabric. "It's just the prettiest dress I've ever seen in my whole entire life."

"Well, I'm not taking it, and I'd rather die than wear it."

"Where'd it come from," Toni pressed.

"Edna Cooper, that's who."

"You're kidding!"

Fannie yanked the gown from her hands. "I am not, and I told her I wasn't going to take it. I don't know why she left it."

Toni grabbed her arm and swung her around. "Wait. What happened? Edna Cooper brought you this lovely gown. The same Edna that used to take breakfast to Blake and Sam every morning until Blake told her to stop?"

"He did?"

"That's what Sam told me. Says he has to eat jerky now unless Mrs. Barnes takes pity on them." She let out a chuckle.

"Why did Blake tell her to stop?"

"Why don't you ask him?" She took the dress back and smoothed it out. "Tonight at the wedding. While you wear this."

Fannie stared back silently. Two things she knew for sure: One, she wasn't asking Blake any such thing, and two, she wasn't wearing that dress.

The rest of the day, the train buzzed with excitement as fires sizzled with cooking meat and women baked as well as they could, parting with enough of their precious provisions to provide several small cakes. A few of the women even deigned to smile in Toni and Fannie's direction. "You see?" Toni said brightly. "All we have to do is give them a little time. Once they get to know me, they'll see I've truly changed my life forever."

Fannie knew Toni was most likely in for heartbreak but didn't want to spoil her good mood, so for once she kept her opinion to herself.

Fannie, dressed in the blue gown she had sworn she was not going to wear, hung toward the back of the gathering as the members of the wagon train watched and listened to the Reverend Cal Smith join four couples in holy matrimony, Edna Cooper and Jason Stewart among them.

The ceremony wasn't the part of the day she'd been looking forward to. Marriage was for foolish women who didn't know any better, and no matter how rosy Toni tried to paint the institution, Fannie wasn't going to be duped into believing a word of it. Marriage was for men. Plain and simple. Women were slaves during the day and at their husband's mercy at night. And she'd never walk down the aisle short of kicking and screaming. At least that's what she told herself as she fought back images of herself dressed in the bride's gown of white, with a wreath of daisies crowning her head like a halo and Blake standing proudly at her side promising to take care of her until death parted them.

She sighed louder than she had intended and nearly fainted in horror as her gaze fell upon Blake's knowing grin not three feet in front of her. She would have run away, but shouts of laughter and clapping vibrated the air as the bride and groom became Mr. and Mrs. Thomas Luther. And she was shoved back and forth as well-wishers made their way toward the couple to congratulate them.

Soon, the moment she had dreaded was upon her, and she stood face-to-face, alone with Blake. She'd avoided him for two weeks. It hadn't been hard to do, as immersed in work as she'd been. But now he stood in front of her, staring down from his six-foot-tall height, eclipsing her easily. "You-uh-got a haircut," she said, then felt like an idiot.

"Sadie did it."

"She did a fine job." Why was Blake suddenly giving her

a moment of small talk? Why was he treating her like he wanted to be around her?

"Good. I figured she would."

Blake seemed just as uncomfortable as Fannie. He had obviously called a truce for the sake of the brides and grooms, so Fannie decided to let him off the hook. "Well, I suppose I'll go help the women with food." She couldn't resist a grin. "We've cooked that cow Mr. Markus finally got fed up with." The animal had run away six times in as many weeks, and his owner had decided to shoot it and offer a feast for the happy couples' celebrations. The gift was much appreciated for more than one reason. The mischievous animal had broken through the wagons and caused damage each time, and everyone's mouth watered for the roasted meat, of which there would be plenty to go around. Fannie had her own reason for wanting the cow dead after it had almost gotten Kip killed.

"Wait, Fannie."

A worried frown creased his brow, and Fannie braced herself for a new fight. "Yes?"

His brown eyes searched her face intently. Fannie drew a breath and held it. What was he thinking? This didn't seem like the same old fight. This was . . . different.

"Blake?"

"I was just wondering, uh, if you would do me the honor of a dance?"

Fannie's eyes grew wide. She slapped her palm to her flushed cheek. "I-I don't think the dancing is starting until after supper."

His own face grew pink. "I meant would you save me one?"

"A dance?"

He scowled. "Well, what do you think I meant? Of course a dance."

"Well, fine, Blake Tanner," she said, raising her voice to match his. "You don't have to get all grouchy about it."

"Fine," he growled back. "I'll see you when it's time for our dance."

"You do that," she snapped, and swung around.

"Fannie, wait."

She stopped in her tracks and looked over her shoulder. "What?"

"You look real pretty in that dress."

Blake stalked away in search of a place of solitude. What was wrong with him? He certainly hadn't planned on asking for a confounded dance. As a matter of fact, he'd wanted to talk to her about Sam's grim news, but seeing the smile on her face as she spoke about the cow took all the thunder from him. And seeing her wearing a dress that brought the blue out in her beautiful eyes had just about made him forget his own name. This just wasn't the time to tell her the bad news. Not before the dance. Not when she was finally letting down her guard even a little.

Fannie tapped her foot in time to a fiddler playing a lively square dance. She refused to give Blake the satisfaction of finding her waiting for his promised dance, so she put on an expression of studied boredom and pretended she wasn't longing to join the dancers in the center of the circle.

Flushed and laughing, Toni flew by in Hank's arms. Fannie envied her. Where was that blasted Blake Tanner anyway? Or was his invitation nothing more than a way to mock her? Tired of feeling conspicuous, she spun around, preparing to stomp off, when someone tapped her on the shoulder.

Relief flooded her, and she turned, expecting to find Blake, apologetic and ready to swing her around the dance floor. Instead, she discovered Willard James. Disappointment nipped closely on the heels of surprise. "May I have this dance, Miss Caldwell?" he asked, bowing gallantly. Behind him, Fannie spied Blake striding her way. A wicked sense of glee rose in her chest. She tucked her hand through his proffered arm. "Nothing would give me more pleasure, sir."

Blake reached her just as Mr. James was leading her to the dance floor. "Evenin', Mr. Tanner," he said, tipping his hat.

"Mr. James." Blake inclined his head. His eyes were stormy as he turned them on Fannie. "Miss Caldwell."

She jerked her chin upward. "Mr. Tanner," she replied with a proud lilt. It served him right to find out she wasn't a woman to be left waiting through three full dances. Let him wait this one out.

The dance, a waltz, began slowly, and Fannie closed her eyes, losing herself in the rhythm. "You dance very well, Miss Caldwell."

Alarm slammed into her at the smell of liquor on his breath. That smell, associated with Tom, always meant trouble. Where had he gotten it? Alcohol was prohibited in the wagon train. Still, she swallowed down her anxiety and tried to keep her voice steady. "Th-thank you. My pa taught me when I was a little girl."

"Ah, the lessons of childhood. You must have had a good upbringing."

Uncomfortable with the direction of the conversation, Fannie said nothing. Willard tightened his hold on her and pressed her close—too close for propriety's sake.

When she tried to pull away, he squeezed her tighter. Anger shot through her, eclipsing fear. "Excuse me, sir. I'm afraid I've become breathless and must sit out the rest of the dance."

"I don't think so. Smile and pretend you're enjoying this as much as I am."

"I insist you turn me loose before I call for help."

"You don't want to do that, Fannie." His smile remained fixed on sensuous lips, but his eyes glittered cold and black as onyx.

Something in his tone told her to heed his warning. This was more than a drunken lecher wanting to dance with a young woman. He had something up his sleeve. "Now, be a good girl and give us a smile. Blake's looking over here like he's about to cut in and rescue his little woman. And I'm not ready to relinquish you just yet."

Fannie painted on a smile as she looked up at the man. "What's this about?"

"I'll tell you in good time, I assure you. For now, I want to enjoy the feel of a pretty girl in my arms."

Recognizing his method of trying to scare her by drawing out the suspense, Fannie tried to relax and form a plan of escape in her mind. She darted her gaze to Blake, but his gaze was fixed on Mr. James and he didn't see the split-second action.

"You don't want to do that," Mr. James said with a cold tone, the smell of alcohol on his breath beginning to turn her stomach.

"Why are you doing this?" she whispered.

"You'll know soon enough. Now, smile at me like you're enjoying our dance."

Accustomed to keeping herself out of trouble through obedience, Fannie showed her brightest smile.

"Good girl." Mr. James gave a short laugh devoid of humor. "We're going to get along just fine."

His prediction seemed dire, and Fannie's heart twisted with dread.

Blake walked by Sam, trying to gauge his reaction to the situation developing in front of them. He purposely avoided staring at Mr. James with Fannie on the dance floor.

"You watching that, Blake?" Sam said in low tones.

"What do you think?" he growled.

"Is she in trouble?"

"I'm not sure what kind, but I think so. I'm trying to decide whether or not to cut in."

"I wouldn't yet. Give him time to hang himself."

As much as Blake hated to admit it, Sam was right. And he wanted the man to go too far. Give him a reason to throw him out of the wagon train. He felt badly for Mrs. James and their children, but the man was bad news, and he had to go.

The waltz finally ended. White-faced and trembling, Fannie left the circle with Willard. The man dropped her back where he asked her to dance in the first place, bowed, and walked off, staggering slightly as he did so. Blake followed him with his gaze. Had the man been drinking? It would be so much easier if he had. That in and of itself would be grounds for dismissal from the train after the incident in Hawkins. And better for Fannie's reputation if she wasn't associated with the scandal in any way. He nodded to Sam, and the scout walked after Willard while Blake went to Fannie. Blake watched her struggle for control, trying valiantly without success to compose her face into a pleasant smile.

"Leave me alone, Blake," she said around a poorly disguised sob.

"You owe me a dance, Miss Caldwell," he said softly.

"Why couldn't you have been here on time?"

"I'm here now." Without waiting for an invitation, he led her to the circle of dancers, slipped his arms around her, and led her in another waltz.

"Do you know what I especially like about you, Miss Caldwell?"

She looked up at him with suspicion. "I didn't realize there was anything you liked about me."

Besides those enormous eyes, now luminous as two pools of pure blue water, there was something else. "Well, you're wrong. There is something."

"What then?"

"I like that you're not one of those women a man has to guess what she's thinking. Your face is as expressive as a child's. And I can always tell what your mood is."

She scowled. "Are you trying to ask me something, Blake? Because skirting around my dance with Mr. James is insulting to my intelligence."

The woman never failed to surprise him. "Fine. What did Willard say to upset you so badly?"

She gathered a shaky breath. "Let's just say, you're about to get your wish."

"My wish?"

"I'll be gone by morning."

Twelve

Toni knew something was wrong the second Fannie left Blake standing alone while dancing pairs flew past him, skirts swirling and boots kicking up dust. Thankfully, Hank had just left her to grab something to drink, so she took advantage of the first moment of peace she'd had all evening and went after Fannie.

When she got within earshot, she called out. "Fannie! Wait for me."

Fannie stopped. Even in the pale light of the night sky, Toni could see that her face was drained of color except for her ever-present freckles. She grabbed the girl by her arms and demanded her gaze. "What happened? Did Blake say something to upset you?"

A short laugh erupted from Fannie's lips. "No. For once, Blake was sort of making an attempt at being charming."

"Then, what's wrong?"

"That's what I'd like to know." Blake walked up behind them. "And what have you been told about wandering around camp alone, at night? It's not safe."

"We're not alone," Fannie retorted. "We're together."

"Have it your way. That's not something I'm eager to argue about at the moment." He walked closer, and Toni dropped her hands from Fannie's arms. "What did you mean, you'd be gone by morning," he demanded.

Toni couldn't hold back a gasp. "What? Fannie, what's he talking about?"

"We're wanted for murder and stealing, Toni."

"How did you know?" Blake's tone betrayed the fact that he already had the information.

The thought must have occurred to Fannie because she slapped her hands firmly on her hips and stared up at him. "How did *you*? Are you planning to turn us in?"

"That remains to be seen," he answered, coolly. "And to answer your first question, Sam found the poster when he went to check out the town ahead of us."

"Poster?" Toni's heart sped up as the answer became all too clear even before Fannie's next words.

"We're on a wanted poster. Both of our pictures, and there's a reward. Mr. James promised me he'd leave you be if I came back to Hawkins with him, quiet-like."

"The reward is five hundred dollars each," Blake said. "Why would Willard agree to such a bargain when he could get double if he took you both?"

"How should I know?" Fannie said with a shrug. "Maybe he doesn't think he can handle the both of us."

Toni still tried to get her mind around the fact that she was a wanted criminal. An outlaw, more or less. "Who are they saying we murdered? And stealing? What is this?"

Blake looked at Fannie for the answers too.

"The wanted poster doesn't give those details," Fannie said. "But I assume they found Arnold's body in that barn. And you and I both took money that Tom and George don't think they owe us."

"Wait," Blake said, stepping closer to Fannie. "Are you saying, you two killed a man and stole from the men you're running away from?"

"No and . . . yes," Toni replied for her. "But George owes me a lot more than I took. He's been spending my money for years while I thought my cut was put up for the day I decided to leave."

"So you weren't there against your will?" Blake asked, a sneer curling his lip.

"Not until I figured I had enough saved to buy some land and start over," Toni answered honestly. "When I told George I wanted to leave about a year ago, he broke the news that I wasn't going anywhere, and, what's more, he never had put back a dime for me."

Blake swung around to Fannie. "What about you?"

"You already know the twins and I were with Tom against our will. For the last year, I've been taking what I figure Tom owes me and the twins for the work we do." Fannie's voice rose with conviction. "I paid us a fair wage but only after the two years of indentured service that our stepfather got paid for were over. I didn't steal a dime."

"What about the murder charge?" Blake asked. "You admitted to knowing about a dead man in a barn."

"The last time we saw him, he was alive and standing on his own two feet," Toni insisted. "Neither Fannie nor I harmed him. I give you my word."

By the skeptical look on his face, Toni could see just how little her word did in convincing him of their innocence. But when he turned to Fannie, his heart was in his eyes. And one thing Toni knew was how to read men. Blake had fallen for Fannie. Head over heels if Toni had to bet on it.

Sam only had to look Willard James in the eye to suspect that he'd been drinking. The stench on his breath pretty much took away any doubt. He had followed the man to his wagon, where Mrs. James had already retired to put her younger children down for the night. Now Willard and Sam stood face-to-face, Willard smiling his false smile and trying to worm his way out of the mess he most certainly had to know he was in.

"What can I do for you, Mr. Two Feathers?"

Sam scrutinized him, unwilling to even pretend to be charmed by the man. "Where'd you get the liquor, Willard?"

"I don't know what you're talking about."

Unmoved, Sam remained calm. "I think you do."

The man's expression turned from friendly to threatening in a flash. "You calling me a liar, breed?"

"Yes."

Willard blinked in surprise, then a smile spread across his face once more. "Well, I guess you caught me. I promise I'll never let it happen again."

Sam nodded. "That doesn't tell me where you got the liquor in the first place."

"Persistent, ain't you?"

Folding his arms across his chest, Sam waited, past the point of being willing to exchange pleasantries with this man.

A scowl marred Willard's face. "All right. I went into town this afternoon. A man needs a drink when his oldest daughter is about to get married. While I was in town, I ran across something real interesting." He reached into his jacket pocket. Sam's hand was on his Colt before Willard could react. "It's not a weapon," he said. "Can I take it out? It's a wanted poster."

Sam's stomach sank. "It's not necessary. I've seen it."

"Ah, so you and Mr. Tanner already know about Miss Caldwell and the whore she's traveling with."

Sam knew the man was baiting him, but he refused to take the bait. "I saw the poster. Whether it's true or not remains to be seen."

"Oh, I see." Willard's face broke into a knowing grin. "Which one are you sweet on?"

"You have two hours to clear out."

"You don't have the authority to make that decision even if you are friends with Blake."

"Talk it over with him if it makes you feel any better, but he sent me to find out if you've been drinking, and he made his position clear. You've been warned before, this is the last straw."

"Fine. I'll clear out first thing in the morning."

"Two hours."

"You can't turn us out in the night," he whined. "What about my youngsters?"

Sam knew the man was simply buying himself more time, but he did have a point. He wouldn't be known as the half-breed that threw a passel of kids out into the night. "Be gone by sunup."

"I will."

Blake posted two guards, including Hank, to stand watch in case anyone tried to sneak into Fannie's wagon and make off with her or any of the others. After making sure they were settled in, he reluctantly turned his footsteps toward his own campfire. He'd prefer to be one of the men standing watch, but as wagon master, it wasn't appropriate. He was responsible for more than just one wagon. From experience, he knew that people would murmur against him if he gave one wagon too much attention.

Sam had already informed him that Willard James would be moving out before sunrise. He knew they'd have to be on their toes for a while, until they had put plenty of miles between themselves and the farmer.

He was just about to spread out his bedroll when the sound of footsteps caused him to finger his Colt as he turned toward the sound. He relaxed his grip at the sight of Mrs. James. Her face was streaked with tears. Blake braced himself against what was sure to come. Obviously, Willard had sent her to plead their case.

"Mr. Tanner?" she said, in a tone barely above a whisper. "May I please have a word with you?"

"I'm afraid I can't change my mind, Mrs. James. Your husband has broken the same rule twice, now. He knew the consequences."

She nodded in understanding. "Yes, sir. I know. You're right. Willard should be punished for breaking the rules over and over again." Her pale face seemed even paler against her black hair, which hung in two braids over her shoulders. She had apparently been preparing for bed when Willard joined her and gave her the news. "I-I want to request that you not punish my children or me for something my husband did."

"What do you mean, ma'am?"

Stepping forward, she grabbed his arm in a viper's grip. "I want to stay with the wagon train and take my children to Oregon."

"Without your husband?"

She gave a vehement nod, her braids bouncing with the movement. "I know you have a policy against women alone. But I have two strong boys who take care of the animals. My girls fetch water for several wagons, and I'm strong."

"I'm sure that's true, Mrs. James, but . . ."

"Please," she pleaded with a hoarse whisper. "I'll do anything to stay. M-My daughter just got married and is heading west. If I leave with Willard, I'll never see her again."

"What's Willard going to say about this?" Blake felt for the woman, he truly did, and he'd like nothing better than to allow her to stay on with the children. But the fact remained that Willard was the rightful owner of the oxen, horses, wagon, and all the supplies. He couldn't force a man out alone on the prairie without his provisions. He'd be as guilty in the eyes of the law as any thief.

She looked down. "He took a horse and left already. Took every cent we had locked away in the false bottom of the wagon. I'll have to take in laundry or find some other way to make money once we reach Oregon. But I don't mind. I'm not afraid of a little hard work."

Blake admired the woman's spirit, but he was focused on the first part of her announcement. Willard had cut out taking everything and leaving his wife and children behind. Anger burned white-hot inside of him. "Mrs. James, you're welcome to stay on."

"Thank you, Mr. Tanner. You won't be sorry. I promise."

"Good night, Mrs. James."

Blake watched her go, reserving judgment. She seemed sincere. But it was just as likely that Willard had orchestrated her request to stay and planned to join her later. One thing he knew for sure. He hadn't seen the last of Willard James.

Thirteen

"Aw, Fannie, none of the other kids do lessons on the trail."

Kip's protests were loud and heartfelt, but Fannie stood firm. "I'm tired of having this argument with you, Kip. You know I promised Mama I'd see to it you and Katie get an education, and I intend to keep to my promise. Now sit yourself down and finish those sums, or you'll be here all day."

"It ain't fair."

"It isn't fair. And you know what? I don't care if every other child on this train is as stupid as a squirrel. You and Katie are going to keep up with your lessons. So put your nose in that book and finish those sums."

And the sooner they finished, the better. Inside the wagon, it was stifling hot. She envied Toni her spot driving the team in the gusty wind that had grown cool over the past couple of hours. She figured a storm was most likely brewing, and longed to sit outside before being driven back inside the wagon to wait out the rain.

"I'm done, Fannie," Katie piped up. "May I walk with Becca?"

Fannie hesitated. Over the past week, since Willard had disappeared from camp, she'd lived in constant fear, despite the fact that Blake made sure guards were posted by her wagon every night. So far, she'd kept the twins close, refusing to allow them out of her sight. But she was beginning to see that they couldn't stay by her side for the rest of the trip. "Be sure Hank is around to watch you walk back to their wagon, okay?"

The little girl's eyes lit with excitement. "Thank you, Fannie."

She leapt for the canvas flap. "Whoa," Fannie called. "Climb up front with Toni and wait for Hank like I said."

"Oh all right." She pouted, but obeyed and crawled back through the wagon. "You never used to make me wait for Hank. I don't see why things have changed all of a sudden."

Fannie had chosen not to reveal the Wanted poster's existence to the twins. There was no reason to make them afraid. "I already told you, Katie. Mr. Tanner is asking us to be more careful than we were in the beginning because it's more dangerous in this part of the country. More Indians, more outlaws, wild animals. He just wants to make sure everyone stays safe. Now do you understand?"

The little girl lifted her tiny shoulders in a shrug. "I guess." She crawled onto the bench by Toni. Fannie stuck her head out of the opening. "I told her she can walk with Becca. Make sure Hank keeps an eye on her, please."

Toni's eyes showed the same concern Fannie felt, but she

nodded just the same. "I see Hank coming back down the line. I'll talk to him as soon as he gets closer."

"Done." Kip's announcement brought a sigh of relief to Fannie's lips. "All right. Hand it over."

"Mr. Tanner said I can ride Peaches and scout with Mr. Two Feathers if you say it's okay. Can I go?"

Fannie hesitated again. "I don't know, Kip. It's starting to rain a little."

"Oh, Fannie. Let the child go," Toni said, her voice filled with tension. "A little rain isn't going to hurt him, and you know well and good Sam won't let any harm come to him."

Fannie considered her friend's words although she couldn't help the tiny bit of resentment that welled up in her at the way Toni undermined her. But she did have a point. She couldn't keep the children locked away out of fear. She made a swift decision. "All right. Be back here before dusk."

"Okay!"

"I mean it, Kip. Don't be late this time!"

Fannie watched Kip until he disappeared up the line, then she turned back to Toni. "What's wrong?"

"Oh, nothing. Just leave me alone."

Hurt jumbled through her. "Have I done something to upset you, Toni?"

The woman's shoulders slumped, and she shook her head. "No."

"Has someone been cruel?"

"No. I can tend to cruel women."

"Don't make me guess, Toni. It's just a waste of energy. Tell me what's upset you."

She gave a jerk of her thumb toward the side of the wagon. "Hank. He asked me to marry him last night."

Fannie gasped. "I thought he was already married."

"He is, Fannie. He wants me to go through with a ceremony by a preacher in front of all the wagon train folks so they'll think we're married after we get to Oregon. H-he says he can't be this close to me every day without being . . . close."

Fannie's face warmed. "You told him no?"

"I was too scared." She shuddered. "He was insistent."

"We're a full week gone from the last town, anyway. There's no telling when we'll find another preacher." Fannie shook the reins to get the oxen's attention away from a piece of prairie grass. "Can't you just sort of hold him off for a while?"

She shook her head. "He wants to ride back on horseback, get married, and rejoin the wagon train within a week."

"But then no one would see you get married."

"I know. I told you, he's unhinged."

And for the first time, Fannie was starting to believe maybe Toni was right. She would always be grateful to the man for helping her leave Tom, but she couldn't bear to watch Toni in such turmoil.

"Toni, you have to come right out and tell him that you aren't going west to build a life with him."

"I know. You're right. But it's not an easy thing to do."

The wind burst across the plain and flung dirt and sand at the wagon train. "Good heavens," Fannie said. "Where did that come from?"

"Look at that sky, Fannie."

Shades of green and black rolled across the horizon. The wagon train came to a slow stop as the rest of the travelers began to realize they were in for a storm.

Blake rode by, his face grim. "We're circling the wagons now. Brace yourselves. This isn't going to be much fun."

"Where's Kip?"

"He's helping get the supply wagon secure. Do you need him to help you?"

Fannie shook her head. "We can do it." She hopped down, and Toni followed suit. They fought the wind and dirt as they began unhitching.

"Fannie, when the storm hits, don't get inside the wagon. Get underneath. With any luck it's loaded down enough to keep from blowing away."

"What do you mean blowing away?" Alarm shot through her. "Are we in for a twister?"

"Could be."

Fannie had lived on the Kansas prairie long enough to be all too familiar with storms. But she'd never seen a twister. The very thought of it filled her with dread.

The two women got the wagon in place and the team unhitched just as the thunder and lightning began to make a terrible show in the heavens.

"Should I get Katie?" Fannie asked just as hailstones the size of dumplings began to rain from the sky.

"Mrs. Kane will see to it that Katie's safe. Let's get under the wagon."

"There's Kip!" The boy ran lickety-split and reached them

in no time flat. "Why aren't you under the wagon?" he demanded.

Kip took his own advice, and Toni followed suit. Just as Fannie was about to join them, the tail of a funnel began to slip from the clouds along the horizon. She watched, mesmerized, as the tail grew wider and longer, swirling and moving and coming straight toward the wagon train.

Blake saw the twister forming and dread hit him full in the gut. He began to question why they hadn't stayed one more day and celebrated the weddings or why they had stopped at all? Either course of action would have allowed the wagon train to escape the impending disaster. But you just couldn't predict these things. Blake was about to slip under the supply wagon when he noticed one person still standing outside, watching the twister form as it headed their way. "Who is that idiot?" he muttered to himself. His heart grew cold as he recognized Fannie's red hair whipping around her head in the wind. "Fannie!" he called. "Get under the wagon!"

She seemed transfixed by the tornado. He'd seen it before. Fascinated terror rendered people paralyzed. The proximity of the twister to the wagon train was troubling, but he couldn't just leave her there. Her tiny body wouldn't stand a chance against the wind as the storm grew closer and closer.

He ran toward her, calling her name, dodging pots and pans and other flying debris.

"Fannie!"

Fannie heard her name, carried on the wind. The twister, fearsome and wild, bore down upon their camp and she knew that this time she really was about to die. "Is that you, God?"

"Fannie! Get under the blasted wagon, you little idiot."

Definitely not the Almighty. The angry shout roused her from her hypnotic state, and she turned to see Blake running toward her.

"Blake!"

"Fannie, get under the wagon."

She dropped to her hands and knees and scrambled toward the wagon. She looked back and, just when she thought her heart couldn't beat any faster, a skillet flew across the camp and slammed into the side of Blake's head. He went down out cold.

Fannie's stomach dropped. She jumped back to her feet and ran the few yards to where the unconscious Blake lay next to Mr. Cooper's empty wagon. Fannie grabbed his arms and began to pull.

"I'm coming, Fannie!" Kip called.

"No!" she shouted back. "Toni, don't you let him set one foot out from under that wagon."

She pulled, her muscles screaming against the burden. "Blake, wake up! Dear Lord in Heaven, please wake him up. I can't pull him alone."

Giving a great heave, she jerked again and again. The wind roared louder and louder, but she was afraid to look up. The force of the gale was so strong now that she had to fight to stay on her feet. If she saw the twister, she knew her courage might fail. And right now, Blake's life depended upon her courage remaining firm.

The rain started in sheets, driving hard onto the parched, dusty earth. It whipped about in the wind until Fannie could barely see. "Blake!" she screamed. Finally, he moved. She crawled under the wagon, grabbed his arms, and tried to pull. "Blake, you have to do this. I can't."

"Fannie?" He turned to the west, and his eyes widened. The twister was so close, only a miracle would keep it from leveling the wagon train. Blake scrambled beneath the wagon and covered Fannie with his body. Hidden in the warmth, Fannie closed her eyes and waited for the end to come.

Blake crawled out from under the wagon and reached down to help Fannie. His head ached and bled, and by the way it spun when he stood up, he figured he had a knot the size of Oregon on his head. Fannie gave a soft gasp as they surveyed the barely recognizable camp. Wagons overturned. Animals on their sides, hurt or dead. Toni and Kip joined them. "I can't believe it," Toni said, shaking her head. "It's just too terrible to believe."

"It looks like the twister hit more directly closer to the end of the train."

And then screams began to fill the air. Blake turned to Fannie. "Are you and your family okay?"

"I have to find Katie," Fannie said. "She was walking with Becca."

"Let's go." He grabbed her hand and pulled her along toward the Kane wagon.

She found Katie sitting alone on the ground. The little girl was staring straight ahead, tears streaming. Fannie rushed to her and gathered her up in her arms. "Thank God you're all right."

"Fannie," Blake said quietly. "Look."

She turned the direction of his gaze. Mrs. Kane sat before the wagon, her arms wrapped around Becca's broken little body. Her face remained stoic, and not one tear glistened on her cheeks. "She was the only baby I had left."

Her weeping husband tried to take her in his arms. "You leave me alone!" she yelled. "This is your fault. I should never have left my home and followed you west. My ma warned me. But I wouldn't listen. Now look. There's nothing left." A strangled sob hit her throat. "Nothing!"

Fannie clutched her little sister tight. That little body could have been Katie. It could have been any of them. Had she really done the right thing taking the twins out of one danger into another?

Fourteen

Blake stood tall on the bed of a nearly empty wagon so that the devastated travelers could all see and hear him.

The terrible news coming from each captain had grown more daunting as the day progressed. Four dead oxen, two horses, two cows, too many chickens to count. Ten wagons had been destroyed. Ten families with no supplies, no shelter. Nothing. How would they survive? The pioneers had been scouring the landscape trying to recover the possessions that had blown across the prairie. The task proved tedious and heartbreaking. Family heirlooms gone in a breath. Life savings taken on the wind and scattered across the plains.

Blake felt completely at a loss, but he knew he couldn't show his uncertainty. Every member of the wagon train looked to him for wisdom, for leadership. For comfort. More so now than twenty-four hours ago. How could he look the grieving Mrs. Kane in the eye and tell her he had nothing to offer? No words to salve the pain tearing her apart?

No one moved as they waited for him to offer . . . something . . . The air was so still he was almost afraid to speak lest his words open the heavens again, like an avalanche on a mountain pass.

He knew he had to say something soon. Looking around the gathering of hundreds, he allowed his eyes to focus and remain on Fannie. She nodded and gave him a shaky smile of encouragement.

"Folks," he said. "We've been through a terrible ordeal in the last few hours." Quickly he went down the list of losses until he reached the human death count. He swallowed hard. How could he tell these people that a quarter of them would have to turn back?

Drawing a shaky breath, he continued. "Eight families have lost loved ones. Little Rebecca Kane. Maury Baker. Ada McCollough." Weeping was heard as he continued down the list of names. Even Blake's voice broke more than once. "Sam?" He turned to his best friend. The scout joined him on the wagon bed. "It's hard to know how to react when something like this happens. The best thing we can do is pray."

Without waiting to ask anyone's permission, Sam closed his eyes.

Toni kept her gaze fixed on Sam. Pray? Did he really think prayer was going to help these people? They had lost loved ones, livestock, their very dreams of a new life. Many of the Oregon-bound travelers had lost so much that they couldn't go on to their so-called land of promise, but they'd never make it back even as far as Hawkins, and there had only been one town between here and that town. The one they'd passed just a week ago. And who knew if the twister had continued its trek of destruction to extend sixty-five miles to the east? What might they find when they reached the small town where only a week ago the pioneers had celebrated happy unions?

Anger built up inside her. How could God do this? These people were guilty of nothing more than hope. And now that hope had been sucked from them in the span of thirty minutes.

Blake took his place at the center of the wagon bed after Sam's brief prayer. "Folks, as I'm sure you've figured out, many of you will not be able to continue. Those of you who have lost half of your provisions, a wagon or your team—even if it was only one ox or horse, come and see me after we break up. The rest of you, please take full inventory and report back to your captain. We cannot go on without the proper provisions to sustain us. I've assigned a detail to butcher the edible livestock. We'll smoke and salt as much as we can to preserve it."

"How long will we have to wait before we can push on?" Mr. Markus called out. "We have to get over the mountains before winter sets in. There aren't nearly enough provisions to keep us through the winter if we have to hole up somewhere."

Murmurs rose from the crowd, quickly becoming a buzz.

Blake held up his hands for silence. "First things first, people. Now I can understand those of you without damage or loss wanting to move on; but remember, the rest of these people are our friends, our neighbors once we reach Oregon. We need to make repairs, clean up, and go from there."

"But how long do you figure?" another man called.

Exasperated, Blake shook his head. "I can't say for sure. But don't expect to move for at least a week. Maybe longer."

"A week!" More groans.

"Look, folks." Fannie elbowed her way through the crowd and climbed into the wagon bed. "Mr. Tanner is doing his dead level best here. Wouldn't you want him to take the extra time if you had lost a loved one or all of your possessions? The best thing we can do is work together and try to get back on the trail as quickly as possible. Tend to your own, then help someone else."

Blake surveyed the crowd, surprised at the calm her words had restored to the weary, heartbroken travelers. He gave her hand a squeeze and let it go as he hurried to reiterate while the folks seemed settled. "Miss Caldwell is right. Tend to your own, then look around and see who needs your help."

Fannie still couldn't believe she'd had the gumption to muscle her way through the crowd and confront the murmuring group, but seeing Blake struggle with his emotions only to have a few impatient men criticize him had just been too much.

Her hand still felt Blake's warmth from the grateful squeeze he'd given her. She shoved aside the quiver in her stomach. There was no time to think about why she felt this way. Why she couldn't understand her reaction when he'd covered her during the storm. Under normal circumstances, she'd have rather faced the twister than be stuffed under a wagon with a man. But it had never occurred to her to fear anything but that storm. Now, she realized how trustworthy he'd been. His thoughts most certainly had been on one thing: shielding her with his body, even if that meant he was hurt in the process—which, thankfully, he wasn't.

When she returned to her wagon, she began the tedious work of taking stock of their possessions. The twister had swung to the right before it reached the wagon train and hadn't directly hit in her section, so she had lost very little. A few pots and pans, the coffeepot, which was a tragedy, but nothing that couldn't eventually be replaced.

By sunset, the day after the twister struck, ten graves were dug, and rocks were gathered to cover each grave to keep out the wild animals. The travelers stood together by lanternlight just beyond their camp and sang "Amazing Grace." Sniffles, sobs, and wails filled the twilight as one by one, folks came forward to speak last rites over their loved ones. To share a bit of the deceased's life, to say a final farewell.

In the absence of a real preacher, the company of pioneers looked to Sam Two Feathers for spiritual leadership, and he rose to the occasion without questioning his right to the position. Fannie watched as he stood by respectfully, silently, and waited for his turn to speak. When the last man walked away weeping after sharing how much he loved his wife of thirty years, Sam clapped the man on the shoulder and took his place next to the gravesites.

"'I am the resurrection and the life, saith the Lord,'" he read. "'He that believeth in me, though he were dead, yet shall he live.' Let us pray."

Fannie couldn't remove the scripture from her mind while Sam asked God to comfort those who mourned and guide each member of the group on their way, whichever direction they might be headed. She wasn't sure she believed in God. It was just too heartbreaking to think that God would take her happy, wonderful childhood, her innocence, and give it to a man like Tom. It was easier not to believe. But who is there to turn to when life gets difficult? And she couldn't help but be comforted that one day she might see her ma and pa again.

The sun hadn't risen high enough to dry off the morning dew when Sam stopped in front of Toni's wagon ready to say good-bye and wish her godspeed as she continued on with the wagon train. Three days had gone by since the twister, and those who were not moving on were ready to move out. Sam would accompany them as far as the last town they passed, then would return to the wagon train. He'd be gone two weeks.

"Hank, I've told you already. I'm not going back."

"But Blythe Creek ain't set up with a blacksmith yet. I could do a right good business. An' yer far enough from Hawkins that no one knows about your past."

"Or yours," she said with a sniff.

"Look, we ain't married in the eyes of the law, me and Running Doe. So you see? There ain't nothin' keeping you and me from gettin' hitched."

Sam knew he shouldn't eavesdrop, but he couldn't pull himself away from the conversation behind Toni's wagon.

"Yes there is, Hank."

Sam frowned. Was that tremble in her voice caused by fear? Or some other emotion?

"What's that?" Hank's voice had grown from cajoling to threatening. Sam remained poised to step in if the need arose.

He heard Toni breathe in as though gearing up for what she was going to say.

"I'm not in love with you."

"What do you mean, you don't love me? What about all them times we was together?"

Sam's jaw clenched at the image Hank's words evoked, and his heart stirred with regret that Toni's life had been so difficult before now. His deepest hope was that she could come to understand the love of a merciful God. He prayed for the woman he was swiftly learning to care for more than he cared to admit.

"You know what those times were, Hank," Toni replied, dropping her tone. "Please don't make me say it outright."

"No. I weren't like all those other men."

"I'm sorry." Toni's voice broke.

"Yer lyin'. Say it! You love me."

Sam stepped forward as Hank's voice rose. He still hung back, waiting, hoping he wouldn't have to step in. But Hank's next words killed any chance that Sam could remain in the shadows.

"Whore!"

Toni's scream sent Sam rushing to her aid just as Hank's blow landed on her cheek. She crashed to the ground. "Hank!" Sam said, keeping his voice as calm as he could, when he wanted to put a bullet through the man's head.

Hank turned on him with a sneer. "Mind yer own business, breed."

"Hank!" Toni's voice filled with outrage. "Don't insult Sam just because you're angry with me."

"Sam, is it?" he spit. "I knowed he was hangin' around you a little too much. Is he one of yer special customers too?"

The last insult was more than Sam could abide. He moved fast, before Hank could respond, and pinned the man's arm behind his back. "I don't like how you're talking to my friend."

"Friend, eh? Is that what they're calling it nowadays?"

"You and your filthy mind better get out of here." Sam turned him loose with a shove away from Toni. In a flash, he lifted his Colt from the holster before Hank could steady himself. The smithy's eyes narrowed as he took note of the weapon.

"Mark my words, girl." He pointed a beefy finger at Toni. "No one makes a fool out of me."

"You made a fool out of your own self," Sam replied. "I suggest you gather your things and clear out."

"That's whut I'm plannin'."

He shoved his hat back on his head and walked away, with the angry gait of a man who wasn't through making trouble.

Toni caught her breath as Sam reached down and pulled her to her feet with strong, steady arms. Emotions she'd thought long buried jumped in her stomach. "Th-thanks, Sam. I'm sorry you had to get involved with that."

"It was my pleasure to come to your assistance, Miss Toni."

That was what she liked about Sam. He never treated her like a prostitute. Even Blake never bothered to precede her name with Miss or call her Miss Rodden. It was always Toni.

But Sam treated her like a lady. She wasn't sure she trusted his respect, but she had to admit she liked it.

"I hope it doesn't cause you any trouble."

His brown face split into a smile. "Don't worry about me."

She returned his smile. "I heard you were leading the wagons headed back to Blythe Creek."

He nodded. "I was coming to tell you good-bye."

Her stomach leapt again. "You were?"

"I know I shouldn't feel this way about you, but before I leave, I just want you to know I am honored to know you."

Toni's lips parted with a quick intake of breath. He shouldn't? She supposed for a religious man like Sam, the thought of caring for a prostitute, former or no, wasn't something his God would likely approve of.

"Honored?" she gave a short, bitter laugh. "You don't have to say that, Sam."

Sam's black eyebrows pushed together. "I don't say what I don't mean."

Unwilling to be made a fool of, Toni kept her feelings in check. How could she have been so stupid as to allow herself romantic thoughts about any man, let alone a man of God?

"Well, I best be getting back and start breakfast." She walked away without waiting for a response. "Thank you for coming to my rescue. I-I hope you don't meet with any trouble during your trip."

"Miss Toni?"

Gathering her courage, Toni swallowed back tears and turned to face him.

"Have I said something to hurt your feelings?"

Toni forced a smile and a short laugh.

"I stopped having feelings a long time ago, Sam. Goodbye."

Fannie saw the confused look of concern on Sam's face as Toni turned her back and walked toward their campfire. "What was that all about?"

Toni shrugged. "Sam's leading the wagons back to the last town we passed. They're heading out in a few minutes."

"I know that. I meant why are you and Sam upset?"

"Hank."

For the first time, Fannie noticed the mark on Toni's cheek, which was beginning to deepen to a purple bruise. The sight fueled her anger. "Did Hank do that?"

Toni nodded. "Right after he told me he loved me and called me a whore."

"I hope Sam flattened him."

Reaching for the only skillet they had left, Toni set it on the fire to get hot. "He didn't flatten him, but he definitely rescued me."

"He cares about you."

Toni nodded. "Yes, but he feels guilty about it."

"What's that supposed to mean?"

"He said he shouldn't care about me."

"Why?"

"Why do you think?"

Fannie drew in a sharp breath. Outrage filled her. "Oh."

Why were men so stupid? "What does it matter what a person used to be?"

"Oh, Fannie. Men want good women to marry and bad women to make them feel manly after the good women become mothers. It's just the way it's always been. Women like me don't get second chances."

"Women like you?"

"Soiled doves, my dear." She dropped bacon into the skillet and watched it sizzle.

If Toni was a soiled dove, what did that make Fannie?

Fifteen

Fannie sat outside the circle listening to the mournful sounds of a lonely harmonica playing "Amazing Grace." Her back ached with the days and days of constant work, and it felt good to sit alone against the wagon wheel and stare into a clear night sky. Alone with her thoughts.

As Blake had predicted, they'd spent a week in camp pulling things back together, and the train would finally be moving out tomorrow. Moving on with over sixty wagons less than a week ago. Between wagons lost, stock gone, and loss of life, folks would turn back to Blythe Creek and settle. For a while at least. Until they recovered enough either to push ahead or turn back for good.

Fannie heard the faint sound of boots on the soft ground. Fannie felt no sense of alarm, and looking toward the approaching figure confirmed there was no need. "Good evening, Mrs. Barnes."

The widow waved her hand. "Please, we've been through

too much to stand on ceremony. Call me Sadie." She planted her hands on her hips and shook her head. "That is one glorious moon, isn't it?"

"It sure is." Fannie patted the ground beside her. "Care to join me?"

Sadie chuckled. "Only if you promise to help me back up if I get stuck down there."

A grin twisted Fannie's lips. The first in a week. It was nice to feel anything other than sadness and loss. "I promise."

With a grunt, Sadie plopped down next to Fannie, sharing the wagon wheel as a back support. She stretched her legs out in front of her.

"What are your plans once you reach Oregon?" Sadie asked.

The thought had been forefront in Fannie's mind for so long, her answer was immediate and without practice. "I plan to claim a piece of land, and Katie, Kip, and I will farm it."

"Supplies cost money. You have what it takes to start up your own place?"

Fannie stiffened. It wasn't her practice to be forthcoming about personal things like finances. But she didn't want to offend Sadie, either.

Sadie patted her leg. "Just tell me it's none of my business, dear heart."

"Oh, no. I didn't mean . . . Well, actually . . ." She hesitated because truly it wasn't the other woman's business. Or anyone else's but theirs, and how would she ever explain the money she had tucked away for safekeeping? Especially when certain people already knew about the Wanted poster and its implication that she was a thief. Was that what Sadie was getting at?

"I'm sure we will make out just fine," she finally said.

"We women have a way of surviving even in the worst of situations."

Something in her tone piqued Fannie's interest. "What will you do in Oregon? Do you have family there?"

"I'm afraid Jesus is all the family I have." She turned to Fannie with a sad smile, half her face shadowed in the darkness of the wagon, the other half illuminated by the moon. The contrast made her sad smile all the sadder, and Fannie reached out without thought and took Sadie's hand. "My husband was killed in a hunting accident ten years ago."

"That's horrible. I'm so sorry." Fannie almost wished she hadn't asked. It wasn't that her heart wasn't squeezed with compassion, but how was she supposed to comfort the woman? "You never had children?" One look at Sadie's face and Fannie knew that was the wrong thing to ask. "I'm sorry, ma'am. It's none of my business."

"It's okay, hon. I don't mind telling you. My Clark and I had three sons. All strapping young things, strong as oxen and twice as stubborn."

Fannie smiled and squeezed her hand.

"A year ago, a bout of cholera swept through our hometown in Missouri. I don't know why I escaped and my boys didn't. When all was said and done, they were all gone, along with about half the town."

"Oh, Miss Sadie. That seems so unfair."

She nodded. "It's easy to blame God when life is unfair."

Fannie's thoughts went to Mrs. Kane and all the other folks who had suffered such tragedy in last week's storm. "Do you ever blame Him?"

"I did." She looked into the night sky as though searching for the face of God.

"No more?"

Sadie shook her head. "I can't lean on Him if I don't trust Him, and I can't trust Him if I believe He took my children."

Fannie's throat tightened as she swallowed hard. "But what if He did?"

"Then I'd rather not know until I stand before Him and see the nail prints in His hands and the love in His eyes."

In the light of such powerful faith, Fannie lost the ability to speak. So she joined Sadie in silence and closed her eyes, trying to make sense of such trust.

Finally, the older woman rustled beside her. "These muscles aren't going to let me sit on the ground any longer, my girl."

Fannie hopped up and extended her arm. Sadie labored to her feet and kept hold of Fannie until she steadied herself. "Thank you," Sadie said.

"A promise is a promise."

Sadie chuckled and reached out, embracing Fannie and turning loose before Fannie could pull back, which she inevitably would have done.

"Good night, Miss Sadie," Fannie said, her throat once more becoming thick as she fought back a rush of unwelcome, unbidden tears.

From within the wagon, she could hear the sounds of Toni getting ready for bed. Katie had fallen asleep long ago, and Kip had started bunking down with Blake, using a bedroll on the hard ground.

She wavered between fatigue and knowing she needed to turn in, what with the busy day ahead of them getting back on the trail after a full week. But she wasn't quite ready to relinquish her solitude. Dropping back to the ground, she once again leaned against the wagon wheel and searched the sky. Was Sadie foolish or wise in her faith?

When she heard the shuffle of feet, she turned with a smile. Sadie must have forgotten to say something. "Look at that smile, darlin'." Willard James grabbed her hair and painfully yanked her to her feet. "You must have missed me."

"Take your hands off me you dirty, stinking skunk," she said, with more bravado than she felt. Rage filled her. How could she have been so careless?

He jerked on her hair, and Fannie fought to keep from crying out. "Don't give me any trouble, little girl. I won't think twice about snapping your neck. Now we had a deal, didn't we? And I expect you to keep your end of the bargain."

"I don't know what you're talking about." Fannie lifted her knee and brought her boot down hard on his foot.

"Ow! You little spitfire. Don't do that again." One fist stayed tightened around a wad of her hair while the other gripped her throat. "You best start remembering."

Fannie scowled. "I'm not going with you now. Not without a fight, anyway. Can't you see we've been through a twister? Don't you even care about your wife and children?"

"Believe me, I've been keeping my eye on them."

"So Mrs. James is in cahoots with you." She gave a bitter, humorless laugh. "Figures."

"Leave my wife out of this and hand over the money."

"I can't get it now, you fool. Everyone's in the wagon, and Toni's still awake."

"That's not my concern."

"Fannie?" Sadie's voice called softly. "Are you still up?"

"I'll be back," Willard whispered in her ear, then turned her loose.

Weak with relief, Fannie leaned against the wagon, her hand flat against her stomach as she fought hard to keep from giving into the dizziness swarming her head.

"There you are." She glanced about. "Is he gone?"

"Wh-who?"

"Willard James, that's who," Sadie said, taking her arm. "Come on, let's go tell Blake."

"Wait! How did you know?"

"I was on my way back to tell you that God was worth the effort to learn to trust, and I saw him. I figured if I called out, he'd run like a scared rabbit, and I was right."

"You shouldn't have taken the chance, ma'am. What if he hadn't run away? He might have hurt us both."

The woman nodded. "I thought of that, but I figured if I took time to get Blake, Willard might have time to hustle you off in the dark, and the men couldn't come after you until morning. By then it might be too late. So you see? I had no choice."

Fannie didn't know what to say. She reached out in an uncommon gesture of affection and wrapped her arms around the plump woman, laying her head against her shoulder. "I don't know how to thank you."

Sadie wrapped motherly arms about Fannie and patted her back like a mother comforting a child. "You just did." She held her out at arm's length. "Now let's go let Blake in on this."

Blake listened to Fannie with a combination of fear, gratefulness, and pure anger.

He wasn't sure which emotion to give in to, so he picked the strongest. "And you didn't even consider maybe I should be informed that Willard was blackmailing you?"

"Mercy, Blake. Don't be so hard on the girl," Sadie admonished. "She's had a difficult enough time without you making it worse."

"I'm making it worse?" he asked incredulously. "She has been nothing but trouble since the second I laid eyes on her."

Deep lines appeared between Sadie's eyes as she scowled. "Except for the seconds she was saving your miserable neck from a twister."

Her words stopped him short. "What's that got to do with . . ."

But Sadie wasn't finished. Nor was she talking to him. Her gaze was firmly fixed on Fannie. "I'd wager he never said a word of thanks, did he?"

"Now that you mention it, no he didn't." Fannie raised her eyebrows and gave him a waiting look.

"Fine. Thank you for pulling me from the path of that

tornado. You saved my neck, like Sadie said."

Although, come to think of it . . . "If memory serves, I wouldn't have been in need of saving if you weren't intent on staring down a storm. I was running to save you and got myself knocked on the head in the process."

"You were?" Fannie's lips parted with surprise. "I don't remember much about that night."

At the sight of her innocent eyes, all the thunder left him. "I called out to you, but you couldn't hear me over the wind. You just stood there, hypnotized by the twister." He remembered the fear he'd felt as though it had just occurred.

"I'm sorry," Fannie whispered. "I almost got you killed."

Blake wanted nothing more than to take her in his arms and reassure her that he was fine. She was fine. They had survived together. But he knew he didn't have the right. She didn't belong to him. Besides, he couldn't quite shake the feeling that she wasn't finished causing trouble for him. If he took her in his arms, the small piece of his heart that didn't belong to her would be lost forever.

"It's all right, Fannie. We both came through it just fine." He cleared his throat. "Now what are we going to do about Willard James?"

Willard rode into the camp where Tom and George awaited him.

"Well?" Tom said around a greasy bite of squirrel. He licked each finger, then swiped the back of his hand over his thick lips.

He turned Willard's stomach.

"Someone came. I had to let her go."

"Did you at least get my money?"

"Not yet. But I will."

"Well, now. I'm having a hard time believing a thing you say, Will," George said, tipping a flask. "This is the second time you've lost the girl."

"I can't help it if the wagon master keeps a close eye on her. I swear I'll get her next time."

"I don't know," George said, staring into the flames. "I think it's time for Clay to move in and get the job done."

Sixteen

As the wagon train left the flat plains of Kansas and entered into the rolling hills near the Platte, the landscape spreading out before Fannie was breathtaking. But as much as she enjoyed the scenery, the oxen struggled with the new terrain, and the wagons were forced to move more slowly, averaging eight miles per day instead of the usual ten to twelve.

Almost a week had gone by since Willard's late-night visit, and Fannie was beginning to think he'd given up, as Blake had once more posted a guard outside her wagon at night. Or was he simply biding his time, waiting to find her in a weak moment alone as he had the other night?

"Fannie?" Katie's sweet voice came up beside her from where the little girl walked alongside the wagon. "I see Mrs. Kane walking all alone by her wagon. May I walk with her?"

Fannie's brow lifted in surprise. "She's out walking?"

Toni swung around and nodded, confirming Katie's observation. "Maybe she's finally ready to face the world again."

"Should I let Katie go?" Since the twister, and the two

incidents with Willard, Fannie had lost faith in her ability to gauge the safety of a situation.

Toni looked at her askance and lifted her shoulders. "I think it might be a good idea for them both."

"Can I, Fannie?"

"I guess. But don't bring up Becca unless Mrs. Kane mentions her first, okay?"

The little girl nodded and climbed out of the slow-moving wagon.

"I wonder why the Kanes didn't go back with the others," Toni said. "If you'd lost your child, wouldn't you?"

Fannie thought of Sadie. She shrugged. "I don't know. Maybe they needed to keep going toward something new. The past might be too painful."

"That's true."

"So, Hank is truly gone, huh?"

"It looks that way. He didn't go with the other wagons when they went back East, though. He must have ridden off alone."

"Are you worried he might come back?"

Toni's lips twisted in a rueful smile. "I imagine he's decided I'm not worth the effort. I only hope he'll go back to his wife and children."

"Me too."

"Fannie, look." Toni pointed across the hills to a lone rider.

"Is it Hank?"

She shook her head. "I don't think so. His horse is black and white. That one's brown." She chewed her lower lip. "I hope Blake or one of the scouts is paying attention." Toni never seemed to feel quite safe.

"You miss having Sam around, don't you?"

"Not really." The words were brave, but by the quick rise of color on Toni's cheeks, Fannie knew she was lying.

She quirked her lips into a grin. "Sure, you don't."

"One man's about the same as another, Fannie. If I miss Sam, it's just because he's the best scout in the wagon train, and we're not nearly as safe without him."

"What about Blake?"

"He has too many responsibilities to keep his attention on the train's safety. Sam's the best," she said, with a finality that brooked no argument. So, for once, Fannie gave her none. It was obvious she cared deeply for Sam. But something had changed between them just before he'd pulled out with the sixty other wagons, and Fannie wasn't sure what. But she didn't feel right about prying, so she kept her curiosity in check. Besides, the rider came closer, cresting the summit of the nearest hill.

"There's Blake going out to meet him."

Fannie's stomach did a turn inside of her. "I have a bad feeling about this."

"Oh, Fannie. So do I," Toni said, the words releasing with a full breath.

The sun reflected off the rider's shirt and Blake had a sinking feeling he was staring at a U.S. Marshal. As the man drew closer, the tin star wrapped in a circle confirmed his suspicion.

The lawman spit a stream of tobacco juice and wiped his mouth with the back of his hand. Blake stiffened. There were two types of lawmen as far as he was concerned. The ones who lived by the letter of the law, serving with integrity and fairness. And the worst sort of character for anyone in authority. The ones who served their own agendas. Blake was willing to reserve judgment for this marshal, but he wouldn't be surprised if the fellow was the latter.

"Good afternoon, Marshal," he said, pulling on Dusty's reins to halt the horse.

The marshal acknowledged him with a nod. Greasy blond hair peeked out from underneath an equally dirty hat. Downwind, Blake had to fight the urge to cover his nose against the man's stench. Another stream of brown juice shot from his mouth. "You the wagon master of this outfit?"

"I am. Is there trouble?"

"That depends on you."

"How do you figure?"

The marshal reached into his vest and pulled out a paper. Blake's heart clenched. There was no doubt what the paper would reveal. The marshal held it out, and Blake recognized the sketches of Toni and Fannie.

"You recognize these women?"

"What if I said no?"

The man lifted one eyebrow and looked over Blake toward the wagon train. "Then I'd exercise my right to search your wagons."

"That's what I figured." Helpless frustration slithered

through him. What else could he do but hand the two women over?

"They're traveling with a couple of children."

"I ain't interested in anyone but those two."

"Give me some time to talk to them and make arrangements for the children."

For a moment, Blake was afraid the marshal would refuse him this request. But after some perusal, the man nodded in agreement.

"You have a half hour."

Blake rode back alone, trying to formulate the words. When he saw Fannie headed out to meet him, he knew he didn't have to break the news to her. She was ready.

Fannie knew by the look on Blake's face that her fears were justified. When he reached her, he swung down from his horse and stopped in front of her. "I guess you figured out what that was about?"

"Who is he?"

"U.S. Marshal."

"Marshal who?"

A sheepish blush crept to Blake's sun-bronzed cheeks. "I didn't even think to ask."

"I guess it doesn't matter." The last time Fannie had seen the marshal come through Hawkins, he didn't look anything like that man. But then maybe they were far enough west that another marshal had jurisdiction.

"Look, Fannie. You're wanted for murder and stealing. Is there anything to either?"

"Definitely not murder."

"Stealing?"

"I told you already. I took what I figure is my fair share and Kip's and Katie's for all the work we did after the two years Silas agreed to."

Blake scrubbed his hand over his stubble. "Oh, Fannie. Your sense of justice might not match a judge's."

"Are you going to just let him take me?"

"I don't have any choice."

Fannie's heart began to beat a rhythm of betrayal so loudly in her ears that she couldn't hear what he was saying. She stared stupidly, wishing she could blame him. Wishing she wouldn't do the very same thing. He had a full wagon train to worry about. She and Toni were two women who, by his own admission, had been nothing but trouble for him since he first laid eyes on them.

"You know," she said. "Hank killed Arnold."

He turned sharp eyes on her. "Hank Moore?"

She nodded. "He was going to take us back to Hawkins. Hank showed up and told us to go on, and he would tie Arnold up and join us to say good-bye."

"So when you left the dead man he wasn't dead?" Hope lit Blake's eyes.

"That's right. And when Hank showed up, he had blood on his trousers."

"Then we need to find Hank."

Fannie's heart sank. "I don't think that's going to do us any good."

"I'll make him tell the truth," he said fiercely. Fannie's heart swelled at the emotional outburst.

"I doubt we're going to find him, anyway."

"Sam could track him."

"Maybe. But Sam's not here."

They fell into silence as they walked the rest of the way back to the wagon train, Blake leading Dusty by the reins.

Toni shook her head when she saw Fannie. "I take it the caller is here to escort you and me to a party."

"Don't make jokes, Toni," Fannie said wearily.

"I'm sorry." She turned her attention to Blake. "Is he taking us back to Hawkins?"

"As far as I know." Blake took hold of Fannie's elbow. "You need to decide what to do about Katie and Kip."

Alarm sucked the strength from her legs, and she stumbled. Blake steadied her within the circle of his arm.

"I can't take them with me?"

"Do you really want to take them back to Hawkins, Fannie?" Toni asked. "Think about where they'd end up."

"Tom."

"Exactly."

Fannie looked down the line of wagons and spotted Katie's strawberry blonde hair. She chattered happily with Mrs. Kane. The woman laughed at something the little girl said and reached out with a full embrace.

In a flash, she'd made her decision. "Wait here." Without staying for an answer, she walked down the line until she came face-to-face with the giggling pair.

"I declare, Fannie," Mrs. Kane said through smiling lips. "Your sister was telling me the funniest story about your pa getting stuck in the chimney."

Fannie gasped. "You remember that, Katie?"

She nodded. "He was trying to pretend he was Santa. Remember?"

"Of course I do." If the child held a memory from when she was only six years old, she wouldn't be likely to forget Fannie.

"Katie, I need to talk to Mrs. Kane for a few minutes. Will you please run along and gather your things from the wagon?"

"What for?"

"I don't have time to explain right now. Please do as I asked."

When she was out of earshot, Fannie gave Mrs. Kane a frank look and included her husband where he sat in the wagon. "Mr. and Mrs. Kane. I have a bit of a problem, and I need help."

By the time she finished her story of their past three years and her fears for Katie and Kip, Mr. and Mrs. Kane had agreed to keep both children.

"If I ever prove I'm innocent, I'll be back for them," she warned.

"We understand."

She gathered a shaky breath as she walked back to her wagon. Blake had had the foresight to summon Kip. "What's wrong, Fannie?" the boy asked.

"Do you see that man over on that hill?" She pointed toward the summit.

The twins nodded.

"He's a U.S. Marshal. Apparently, they found Arnold dead and think Toni or I or both of us killed him."

"I won't let him take us back!" Kip said.

"Oh Kip," Fannie said sadly. "I don't have time to argue with you."

But Kip wasn't done. He swung around and faced Blake with fury. "Why are you letting him take us?"

Fannie grabbed his arm to get his attention. "Listen to me. I mean it. Blake doesn't have a choice. What do you want him to do, shoot a marshal?"

"But we didn't kill anyone."

"I know. And hopefully the judge will believe us." Fannie didn't hold out a lot of hope for that particular miracle.

"This is why you wanted me to gather my things?" asked Katie.

"Yes, baby."

"Are they going to put us in jail?" the little girl whispered, her eyes filled with fear. Fannie reached out and embraced her, holding her tightly. "The marshal isn't here for you and Kip, sweetheart."

"Good," Kip said. "I'll break you out of jail."

"You're not coming with us," Fannie said flatly. "The Kanes have agreed to keep the two of you until I get back."

The twins set up a howl of protest to put a pack of coyotes to shame. "That's enough, you two. I can't look after you if you come. Do you really want to go back to Hawkins and have some judge give you right back to Tom?"

Katie shook her head.

"Well, I don't want that either."

"I ain't staying."

"You are. And that's the end of it, Kip. We only have about ten minutes left. Do you want to spend it arguing?"

"No."

"All right. Get inside and gather your things and move them to the Kanes' wagon."

For once the lad obeyed. Fannie turned to Blake. "I need to speak with you alone."

Toni placed an arm around Katie's shoulders. "Come on, Katie. Let's go make sure you have everything you're going to need."

When they stood alone, Fannie sized him up, hating that she was in a position to trust someone. But she had no choice. "I want you to look after the twins' money."

Blake frowned. "I don't know if that's such a good idea, Fannie."

"You're the only one I trust. I don't know the Kanes well enough to hand over a few hundred dollars. They might squander it on their own land or things that don't matter. I want it put aside for the twins so that they have a future."

Fannie hated to beg, but the very fact that he hesitated proved he was the right man for the role of godfather for the twins. "Please, Blake. Don't I have enough to worry about without adding this to the list?"

His eyes softened. "All right, Fannie. You have my word. But if you're not back by the time we reach Oregon, I'll head back over the mountains to find you."

At the fierce honesty of his vow, Fannie's pulse quickened. "You will?"

He nodded and moved closer, but stopped at the sound of Kip's voice. "The marshal's headed this way."

Fannie turned to the hills. She jumped into the wagon, found the money bag, and shoved it into Blake's hands. "You promised."

He nodded. "I promised."

She turned to the twins. "Come here, Kip and Katie. Quickly."

Wrapping them both in her arms, she fought hard not to weep.

As she held them, her gaze fell on Blake's. There was no mistaking the passion in his eyes. The utter helplessness. "Look after them, Blake."

He stepped forward and put his arms around the three of them and held them tight. "You have my word."

Seventeen

Fannie kept her gaze straight ahead as the wagon rolled away from Kip and Katie. The marshal rode alongside the wagon with his rifle slung carelessly over the saddle, aimed straight at Fannie's head.

Her thoughts remained on Katie and Kip. She had some measure of relief knowing that they would be well cared for. But her heart ached at the thought of never seeing them again. She and Toni knew they were innocent, but without Hank's confession, there was no way to prove it. How would they, two women of scorn, ever convince a judge to take up their cause?

So she truly didn't care that the sneering marshal seemed to delight in cocking and uncocking his rifle. Let the gun go off and send a bullet crashing through her skull. After the three years she'd just endured, only to escape and be recaptured, she welcomed a swift ending to a miserable existence.

When they'd been on the eastward trail for close to three

hours, the marshal ordered Fannie to veer off the road. "Why should I do that?" she asked.

"Because I'm the one with the gun, and I'm tellin' you to."

"You told Blake you were taking us back to Hawkins."

The marshal shoved the rifle against the side of Fannie's head. "I'm not arguin' with ya, girlie. Do as I say."

"Just do it, Fannie," Toni said, her voice weary and defeated. "It's not worth dying over."

"Better listen to your friend, here," he said. "She's talking sense."

But Fannie wasn't so sure. "Why should we veer off the road and head in a completely different direction from Hawkins? That makes no sense."

"Because," Toni said. "As he pointed out, he's got the gun."

Something wasn't quite right with this so-called marshal. Fannie couldn't put her finger on it, but he seemed more outlaw than lawman. What if Tom had sent him? She shook her head. It was just too ridiculous. Tom didn't have the brains to come up with that sort of plan.

Against her better judgment, she turned the oxen away from the trail, praying she wasn't making a big mistake. But with the rifle pressed menacingly against her temple, Fannie felt she had no choice. She had to think of a plan, and thinking would be a lot more difficult with a bullet in her brain. As much as she might welcome an end, her sense of duty rose to the surface, and thoughts of Kip and Katie growing up without her spurred her decision to fight.

* * *

Blake couldn't shake the feeling that something wasn't right. The entire wagon train lumbered forward with morose silence. Or at least that's the way it seemed to Blake. Maybe it was his own foul mood, but it seemed to him that the atmosphere itself leaked ill tempers and tension.

Katie, who had adored Mrs. Kane before Fannie was taken away, now couldn't bear to be in the same vicinity. She openly defied the woman and had run to the front of the wagon train to find Kip, where he rode Blake's second horse, Shane. They now rode double on horseback. And no one had the heart to reprimand Katie for running off or Kip from welcoming her on his mount when every extra pound on a horse's back in this heat and with these hills only made it that much harder on the animal.

At noon, Blake called a one-hour lunch break. The sun beat mercilessly, and most folks didn't feel like eating anyway, so the typical fare was jerky and cold beans left over from the night before. Otherwise, quick corn cakes, biscuits, or anything else that could be served cold. It was definitely a small meal any way you looked at it.

Kip and Katie sat nibbling at molasses-soaked leftover biscuits, their miserable silence leading Blake to wish he was better at talking. Times like this, Blake missed Sam. His friend would have known what to say to make Kip and Katie feel better. But Blake felt at a loss as the two came to him, and not the Kanes, for their noon meal.

Finally, movement from the corner of his eye caught

Blake's attention as Katie nudged her brother. Kip swallowed nervously and looked at Blake.

"Something on your mind, Kip?"

The boy nodded, swallowing down a bite. "Katie and me was wondering if we can take Shane and go swimming in the creek Grant Kelley mentioned when he came back from scouting."

"I don't know if that's such a good idea, son," he said.

"The Kanes already gave their permission if you said it was okay."

Now, that surprised Blake, but Mrs. Kane would probably agree to just about anything to gain Katie's love after losing her own daughter so recently.

Grant Kelley, a former sheriff with troubles he hadn't seen fit to share, had proven himself invaluable as a tracker since Independence, and Sam had put him in charge of the rest of the scouts in his absence. Grant had come back with news that the creek was at least five miles away. Not a long ride on horseback, but these days, it would likely take the wagon train the rest of the day to reach it, and they'd make their evening camp alongside the creek. "I see. The two of you thought you'd ride on ahead, take some time to frolic in the water, and wait for the rest of us to get there?"

Kip gave him a guilty grin that nearly did Blake in. "Yes, sir. I like to practice every time we come to a river or a creek." He'd taught the children to swim before they left the banks of the Big Blue River. He was taking no more chances that they would drown because of something as silly as the absence of a skill every child should have by the age of four.

Still, the pair were new swimmers at best and could get into trouble with a strong undertow or miscalculating distance from one bank to the next. He hesitated to give permission, regardless of the Kanes. "I'm not sure it's such a good idea, kids."

"Oh, Blake," Sadie broke in. "What will it hurt to let them have a little fun? They probably need to get off by themselves for a bit to think things through. And if Mr. and Mrs. Kane already gave their permission . . ."

"Yeah," Kip said, his eyes soulful and watery. "We miss Fannie an awful lot."

There really wasn't a good excuse not to allow a little swimming excursion on such a hot day. Their scout, though admittedly not as capable as Sam, still had a good nose for trouble. He'd reported no signs of wild animals between here and the creek. And no Indian activity. After a couple of more seconds, Blake looked from one child to the other. "All right. I reckon the two of you deserve a little fun. But be on the lookout for signs of danger."

There were no shouts of excitement, no exclamations of thanks, but Blake understood. These children had lost so much already. Losing Fannie had been as devastating as their parents' deaths. For all intents and purposes, she'd filled the role of mother, father, and older sister. The void left in her absence couldn't be filled by a simple outing.

He watched as they hurried to Shane. Kip climbed up first, then swung Katie up, settling her behind him before lifting his hand in farewell to Blake. They rode away at a gallop, Katie's braids flying behind her in the wind.

His thoughts turned to Fannie. He was surprised at the void she'd left in his life as well. Larger and blacker than he'd ever thought possible. He'd always considered himself a loner. Even thoughts of needing a wife were more for practical reasons than the desire for companionship. But after coming to know Fannie, he could imagine his life with only one woman. How could he sit across the table from another female with less-than-perfect wide blue eyes? Perfect, crazy, unruly hair that refused to stay put beneath pins or wrapped in braids?

"I know." Sadie spoke up. "I miss her too."

Blake didn't even try to deny who he'd been thinking of. As a matter of fact, Fannie was the only thing on his mind, and he hadn't slept a wink in well over twenty-four hours. He was exhausted, lonely, and wishing that marshal had never caught up to them.

"Something's not right." Toni's whispered words weren't news to Fannie. She'd spent the last several hours trying to figure out how to overpower the marshal and hightail it back to Katie and Kip and Blake. She hoped the problem was a simple matter of the fool not realizing that by veering off the main trail, they'd be taking a long way around to get to Hawkins and were probably lost. Maybe his was a case of stubborn pride incapable of admitting he didn't know where they were.

"Marshal?" she asked, her voice a startling contrast to the silence of the treeless landscape.

"What?"

"It's going to be dark real soon."

"Don't you think I got eyes? Just shut up and keep going."

Fannie gave an exasperated sigh. "Listen, I haven't eaten all day. And I need to . . ." She broke off. Even in these dire circumstances she couldn't bring herself to mention nature's call by name. "You know . . ."

"Need to what?" he asked.

"Good heavens," Toni spoke up. "What do you think?"

"Oh. Well, why didn't she just say so?" He pulled his horse to a stop. "I could use a stop myself. You got five minutes."

Toni moved to exit the wagon. Fannie halted her with a hand on her arm. "Kip's gun is in the wagon."

Toni's eyes grew big. "Where?"

"Under my pallet, I saw him put it in there right before the marshal reached us. But if I don't climb down and . . . you know . . . he'll get suspicious."

"What are you two whispering about?"

"Now, Marshal," Fannie said, trying to sound like a fainting, foolish woman. "There are certain things a woman doesn't share when a man is in earshot. Private woman things."

He cleared his throat with nervous embarrassment. "Well, stop that chattering about private things and get to it, or you'll just have to hold it until we reach camp."

She climbed down from the wagon and walked around to the back for some privacy. When she finished, she only prayed Toni was able to take advantage of the marshal's own need to relieve himself and grab the pistol from the back when he wasn't looking.

Toni nodded as Fannie climbed back into the wagon. The pistol sat on the seat, beneath the folds of Toni's skirts.

"Did you notice the marshal said when we reach camp, like we're meeting with someone else?"

"Yes," Toni whispered. "I have a bad feeling about this."

"So do I."

Fannie gathered her breath and did what she knew she should have done hours before. *Please God,* she prayed silently. *We need your help.*

A broken axle had delayed the wagon train for a good two hours. Knowing Kip and Katie were alone with no food and darkness closing in, Blake pressed on, cursing himself for being stupid enough to let a couple of kids ride off alone. Especially kids who had only recently learned to swim.

His thoughts turned to Mrs. Kane, and he whipped Dusty around in a split second. The woman must be sick with worry. When he reached their wagon, he removed his hat and nodded a greeting to the couple sitting side by side on the wagon seat. Mrs. Kane smiled a sad smile in greeting. He supposed that melancholy would be around a while. Not that he blamed her. It must be horrible for a mother to lose a child. Most mothers anyway.

"Good evening, Mr. Tanner." Mr. Kane kept the horses moving. "Glad to be moving again. I take it the repair was made."

"Not entirely. We need a blacksmith. But it'll hold for now."

"That's good."

Awkward silence filled the space between them. Blake cleared his throat. "Just wanted to let you folks know we should be at the creek in a few minutes. We'll be circling the wagons soon. I figure Kip and Katie will likely ride out to meet us within a few minutes."

A frown touched Mrs. Kane's brow. "What do you mean? I thought they were riding with you today."

"They did before lunch. But they rode on ahead to swim before the rest of us got to the creek."

Mr. Kane slipped his arm about Mrs. Kane's shoulder and stared at Blake with an accusing glare. "Why would you allow them to go off alone without seeking our permission? I realize they're not our children, but we've agreed to raise them in Miss Caldwell's absence. I think that entitles us to the same consideration their mother and father might have been given if circumstances had been different."

A dozen different thoughts swirled through his head at once. Possible explanations. Until finally only one explanation made real sense. Cold sweat trickled down his spine. The children had obviously lied to him. "I don't know how to say this, but Kip told me you had already given permission if I said it was all right. So I made a judgment—a poor one, I recognize—based on what I thought you wanted."

Zach scowled and gave him a look that made Blake squirm. "Mr. Tanner," the man said. "My wife lost our little girl such a short time ago. Why would we allow these children to wander off alone when we're so desperate to keep them close? Mrs. Kane has been struggling against tears all day, and I was very close to bringing them both back to our wagon before we made camp just to give her peace of mind."

Suddenly Blake's collar seemed awfully tight. How could they have lied to him? When he caught up with those two, he'd show them a thing or two. They were both going to work so hard at extra chores that they wouldn't have time to get into trouble.

"I apologize for not thinking through the possibility they might be lying." Real remorse filled him. "I've never had much dealings with youngsters."

"We understand, Mr. Tanner," Mrs. Kane said. "But please come to us from now on when the children ask to do something potentially dangerous from a parent's perspective."

Blake slapped his hat back on his head. "I give you my word." He kicked Dusty's side and rode up the line until he found Grant Kelley. "Grant, the kids lied. They weren't given permission to go swimming today. I'm afraid they might be scared or something worse."

A crooked grin split the tracker's face. "Those little scallywags. Imagine them telling a lie just so's they could get a dip in the creek ahead of the rest of us."

"Yeah, imagine." Blake wasn't even close to amused by the twins' antics, and he intended to give them each a few choice words as soon as they showed up.

"You want me to ride on ahead and find them?"

"Yeah. And make them stay put."

"Yes, boss."

Eighteen

Fannie reached for the pistol sitting on the seat between her and Toni. She fingered the cold steel, trying to decide if now was the time to use her ace in the hole. One thing Tom had taught her, there was a time to hold back and a time to play your hand. Of course, Tom had lost his shirt nine times out of ten, so she wasn't so sure anything he taught her was much good.

Their escort had become more talkative during the last half hour, his spirits much improved, like Tom after a shot or two of whiskey on a cold winter night. But Fannie hadn't noticed a bottle, so she could only conclude that his change in demeanor was a result of knowing they were getting close to meeting up with his partners or deputies or whoever they were supposed to meet. One thing was certain, the marshal wasn't going it alone.

But how close were they? If she didn't make a move soon, it might be too late. No telling how many men would be in camp once they arrived. Might be one—and one she could handle—or it might be a hundred, and no way she could stave off that many men with one six-shooter.

Toni nudged her and nodded for her to do it. "Double over like you're sick," Fannie whispered. She pulled on the reins and halted the oxen just as Toni picked up on her cue and started moaning like a woman in labor.

"What do you think you're doing, girl?" The marshal's voice was gruff and threatening.

"Something's wrong with Toni."

"What's wrong?"

"I-I can't say," Toni said, groaning and moaning like death was imminent. If not for the seriousness of their present circumstances, Fannie would have laughed and laughed.

"I think you best take a look at her, sir."

"I ain't no doctor," he growled. "Git movin'. There ain't nothin' we can do about it for now."

Taking a chance the man wasn't who he said he was, Fannie tried a bluff—another card-playing tactic Tom was no good at.

"I thought all lawmen received some medical know-how before they were sworn in."

He gave her a stupid look that, in the light of his lantern, looked downright comical as he tried to figure out how to respond.

"Well, we are taught a little doctorin', but mostly I ain't very good at it."

Toni's wails grew louder and more pathetic. Less convincing to anyone with half a brain, but apparently the so-called marshal lacked in that department.

"I reckon I could take a look."

"We'd appreciate anything you can do for her."

He swung down from his horse, his rifle firmly in his hands. He frowned as he looked Toni over, clearly trying to decide if he ought to touch her or not. "You-uh-say yer innards are ailin'?"

Toni nodded, her face twisted in agony. "What do you think it might be?"

He slipped a hand across the stubble on his cheek as his perplexity about the situation clearly overwhelmed him.

"Maybe you ought to take a look, sir," Fannie said, tossing in the "sir" to throw him off the scent.

He nodded with self-importance. "Maybe you're right." He took a step up on the side step of the wagon.

Fannie knew it was now or never.

In a flash, she whipped the pistol from its hiding place and shoved it inches from his nose. Surprise widened his eyes. Then fear as Fannie turned her lips upward in a smile that clearly bespoke the change of events. "Drop the rifle, Marshal." He did so. "Now back down, slowly. Hands up!"

He complied.

"Nice job, Toni." She grinned. "You could have been an actress on the London stage."

Toni laughed out loud. A beautiful sound after days of heartache.

"No thank you," she said, climbing from the wagon. "Finding a nice husband and settling in the West will suit me just fine."

It was apparent their captor turned captive was starting to realize the situation he now faced.

"Where'd you get that gun?"

"Only a fool doesn't check a person's personal belongings before they kidnap them. And no U.S. Marshal is that big of a fool, *Marshal*. Who are you really?"

"I don't have to tell you nothin'," he said, a sneer curling his lips.

"Now, Clay, there ain't no call for rudeness."

Fannie turned as a hulking shadow appeared from behind the wagon.

"Yeah, Clay," another voice, tinged with amusement, echoed. "No call for rudeness."

Dread turned over in Fannie's gut. Toni uttered a groan—a real one this time, and Fannie knew her friend's despair rivaled her own. The voices were all too familiar. Only God could help them now.

Blake fought to keep his panic in check as Grant reported back twenty minutes after riding out after the children. "No sign of them, Blake."

"What do you mean? Did you look all up and down the creek?"

"It ain't that big. And it ain't deep enough to drown two kids and a horse with no sign, if that's what you're wondering."

Relief washed over Blake that he hadn't been forced to ask. To voice his fears the children had escaped the waters of the Big Blue River only to drown in a creek because he'd been foolish enough to send them off alone. "Do you think they were lost?" Or please God no, captured by Indians, killed by wild animals?

Grant shook his head. "I did some looking around. They never made it to the creek at all. I suggest we take a few men first thing in the morning and double back."

First thing in the morning? They could be dead by then. Or hurt, or scared. Fannie would never forgive him if he let anything happen to those twins. They were everything to her. All she had in the world, and she had entrusted their well-being to him. Their futures. And what had he done? Put them in probable danger by being an idiot.

"You're not thinking of going out in the dark?" Grant asked.

"It crossed my mind."

"I'd advise against it."

"I can follow the wagon trail back to where we stopped for our noon meal and make camp. I'll be that much closer and should be able to pick up their trail at first light."

"Should I tell Vern Cooper to keep an eye on things until we get back?"

"We?"

"You can't go alone. It's not a good idea, being as how you're the wagon master and all. If something happens to you, we're in big trouble."

The former sheriff was smart. And had a point. "I'd appreciate the company."

While Grant prepared Vern Cooper and the rest of the train captains for Blake's absence, Blake made a stop at the

Kanes' wagon. He dreaded telling Mrs. Kane that the children were missing but knew the news needed to come from him.

She began to weep as soon as the first words were out of his mouth. "I knew it. I just knew it was too good to be true. I'm just not meant to be a mother."

Vern placed an arm around his wife. "We've lost four children, Mr. Tanner. Three to illness and Becca." His voice broke. "We thought God had given us another chance. But . . ."

"Don't give up." A surge of determination shot through Blake. He would most certainly bring back those children and, after a good reprimand, he'd turn them over to this couple who would love them as much as any child had ever been loved. Fannie had made a good choice.

Fannie's wrists burned raw and red from the tight ropes binding her hands together in front of her. She stumbled as Tom led her into camp by a leash. Toni wasn't faring much better as George shoved her forward.

If only she had waited a few more minutes to reveal the gun. There were only George, Tom, Clay—the pseudomarshal—and one other man, who remained in the shadows as they entered the camp. Clay had tied his horse to the back of Fannie's wagon and drove the oxen himself, taking no chances Fannie had something else up her sleeve.

Tom shoved Fannie to the ground and tied the rope around her middle, firmly securing her to the wagon wheel. George followed his example with Toni. Thankfully, he secured her on the same side of the wagon as Fannie. They were on the side of the wagon closest to the fire, so no wild animals would venture close.

Tom stuffed a filthy handkerchief in her mouth. "How do you like being tied up and gagged?"

Wishing she could call him every name that entered her mind, she gave him a steady glare.

"Well, now," he mocked. "Don't have nothin' to say?"

She had plenty to say if the coward would take this foul handkerchief out of her mouth. Anger eclipsed fear at the thought of Tom's getting the better of her. The idiot couldn't even balance his own books, and yet he'd devised a plan to capture her. One that even Blake had fallen for.

"What are you planning to do with us?" Toni asked.

George gave an evil chuckle. "That's gonna depend on you, now ain't it?"

"On me?"

"I lost me a bunch of business when you left. Yer gonna be workin' day and night to make it up." He squatted in front of her and took her chin in one palm. "Where's my money," he hissed.

Toni jerked her head up and said, "I don't know what you're talking about."

Fannie watched in horror as he reared back and struck with such force that Toni's head slammed against the wagon wheel.

Without thought, Fannie fought against her bindings, twisting, her raw throat issuing a scream behind the gag.

"Now, look. You have Fannie all upset," George said, his fist wound around Toni's hair. "The money."

"I don't have it anymore."

"What do you mean?"

"I gave it away before your fake marshal kidnapped us."

A guttural roar bellowed from George. "You gave my money away?"

Toni's lips curved ever so slightly, and even as they did, Fannie's heart filled with dread. "Every last cent."

Toni didn't so much as flinch as George drew back his fist and unleashed his fury.

Helpless horror overwhelmed Fannie and tears of anger welled up inside of her. One word repeated over and over in her head as George meted out his punishment with more force than anyone should have to endure: No! No! No!

When Toni's head finally lolled in unconsciousness, George pulled back, his breath coming in gasps.

Tom turned to her. "Is my money gone too?"

She nodded, bracing herself for the same punishment Toni received. Instead, Tom turned to the man in the shadows. "This is yer fault, Willard. If you'd got hold of her the first time. Or the second time ya had her, I'd have my money."

Fannie fought her nausea as Willard James stepped out of the shadows. He stared at Fannie. "Told ya I'd see ya again."

Tom gave him a shove. "Don't sound like you had anythin' to do about it. Because of you, I'm missin' my money and the other two."

The twins. Fannie should have known he wouldn't be satisfied with just her. He wanted Kip and Katie back too. After all, one slave wouldn't suffice when a man was accustomed to three, she thought with outrage. Bitterness.

Then a thought struck her. They were still wanted. She thought of the poster with the images of herself and Toni sketched onto the paper. Grim satisfaction sliced through her. Tom might not get the pleasure of her company for too long. Because the first real lawman she came across, she intended to turn herself in. Better to face the end of a noose than life with that stinking, miserable pig.

The men soon began to pass a flask back and forth between them. They kept the fire low and ate jerky. Fannie swept her gaze to Toni. Her bruised, bloodied face nearly broke Fannie's heart. She prayed for the only friend she'd ever had. *Please, God. Don't let her die.*

Their plight had been dire enough when it appeared they'd be facing a judge for a crime they hadn't committed. But to be sentenced to a life in Hawkins with these two men would be worse than before. Especially if Toni's present condition was an indicator of what was in store for them.

Still, she couldn't help but feel a measure of satisfaction that the twins were safe. She closed her eyes, picturing them snug within the Kanes' tent, sleeping soundly, bellies filled and loved.

Life would have been wonderful if their plan had worked out, and they had reached Oregon together, but for this one small favor, she would be ever thankful to God. She vowed that for the rest of her life, however long or short, no matter if she hung for murder or remained Tom's captive, she would picture smiles on the twins' faces and remember that their happiness was well worth her sacrifice.

* * *

Blake found where the twins had doubled back after barely heading toward the creek. How on earth had they gotten past every scout and lookout in the wagon train? Not to mention himself? The only thing he could figure was that the distraction of the broken wagon axle had given them just the opportunity they needed to slip by undetected.

Fannie's body ached miserably as the sun burned through the top of her head and her mouth begged for something moist. The drunken fools had stayed awake laughing and mocking and feeling very pleased with themselves. Tom appeared to have forgiven Willard for being inept, and the two did a little jig sometime after midnight. The sun had been up for hours, and still, all four lay close to cold ashes where the campfire had long since died.

"Psst."

Fannie swung around, her heart leaping. Toni? She frowned. Toni's eyes were still closed—unconscious, sleeping, or . . . Her chest rose and fell, to Fannie's relief. Just as well she remained unconscious. The pain would probably be more than she could bear if she woke up.

"Psst. Fannie."

She twisted enough to look behind her. Kip! Katie! What in blazes were they doing?

Kip stayed low and slithered close while Katie hung back, hiding behind the wagon wheel on the other side of the wagon. Kip reached her swiftly and took the gag from her mouth. "What are you doing here? Where's Blake?"

"Shh." Kip frowned and went to work on the bindings.

"I mean it, Kip. What are you doing here?"

"We ran off. Blake thought we were going swimming."

"Kip, you have to stop trying to untie me. You're never going to get them loose without a knife anyway. Go get help."

"I'm not leaving you." His brows pushed together in fierce determination.

"You have to. Listen to me. Toni's hurt real bad, and I can't sneak off and just leave her here. If you go back and get Blake, at least he'll know the marshal wasn't a real marshal."

"You come with us, Fannie," Katie said, her voice trembling. "Let's go get Blake together."

"Honey, you two need to go now, before the men wake up."

"Well, if this ain't just like Christmas. Lookee what Santa brung me."

Fannie groaned at the sound of Tom's voice. "Run!"

"Don't do it," Tom shouted. He pointed his rifle at Fannie's head. "She's dead if you run."

"I think Sam trained that boy a little too well," Grant said, amusement thick in his voice. "Look, he tracked the wagon off the trail."

"I wonder why the marshal took the women away from the trail," he mused aloud. By the time the afternoon gave way to twilight, it was all too clear. Other tracks joined the wagon's, and Blake's stomach sank lower and lower.

"They're in trouble," Grant said grimly.

"We have to find them." A sense of urgency swept Blake. He had a feeling if he didn't find them before another night passed, not all of them would make it back to the wagon train alive.

They knelt on the ground examining the tracks to gauge the situation when the grass crunched behind them. Blake swung around. How on earth had two trackers allowed themselves to be taken by surprise?

Fannie grabbed the canteen of tepid water with both hands. Tom still hadn't given them anything to eat, but at least he'd finally given them water. "I went a whole day without water," he said. "How'd it feel?"

She didn't bother to answer. All she knew was that her plans had changed. She couldn't turn herself in to the nearest lawman when Kip and Katie were in Tom's clutches along with her.

Nineteen

Blake's relief knew no end as he stared into the face of his best friend. "Sam! I thought you'd be gone at least another three or four days."

"We finished up sooner than I figured."

"I'm going to scout the area while the two of you catch up," Grant said.

"Good idea. We have to be getting close."

When Grant was gone, Blake turned to Sam with puzzlement. "What are you doing here?"

"Caught wind of a couple of fellows who had bragged about a scheme. The saloon keeper and storekeeper from Hawkins worked together to make us think Toni and Fannie are wanted by the law."

"What do you mean?"

"Barnabas went into the saloon and started up a conversation with a fella. When this man found out Barnabas was from our wagon train, he started talking about a couple of men who were bragging about how their women had left them, but that they were going to get them back."

Blake's heart nearly stopped. "You think Tom and George have the women?"

Sam gave a solemn nod. "But it's worse than that."

"How?"

"The Wanted posters were fake. They made two and took them to Blythe Creek because that was the next town we were likely to stop. When they saw me, they paid a man to be sure I saw it."

"And we fell for it." Blake felt like a fool all over again. Condemnation whittled away at his confidence until he felt like something less than a man.

"So," he said, "if the posters were fake, that fella back at the wagon train wasn't a U.S. Marshal."

"Looks that way."

"How'd you know where to find us, Sam?"

"Before they left town, Tom and George let it slip that they'd be camping out south of the trail waiting for their partner to bring the women. I followed the trail until I saw the tracks that veered off and took a chance."

"All right. We know Fannie and Toni are with the two men. But maybe we can get to the twins before they catch up to them."

"The twins?" Sam asked.

"I'll explain on the way."

Grant came back into view. "We're close like you said. Their camp is over the next hill. I suggest we go the rest of the way on foot."

* * *

Fannie was growing more and more concerned about Toni. She had yet to regain consciousness, and she looked so bruised and broken that Fannie feared she was close to death.

"Tom," she called.

It was already noon before all of the men awakened, and the lazy ne'er-do-wells had decided to remain in camp another day. Fannie was relieved that Toni wouldn't have to endure a wagon ride. Still, it was heartbreaking to see her slumped over. George insisted she remain tied up even though she hadn't moved.

"Tom!" she repeated.

"What do you want?" His words were already beginning to slur.

"Tell George that Toni's going to die if she doesn't get some water."

"She's unconscious. She won't be able to drink it."

"Let me help her. You know I'm not going to go anywhere and leave the twins here alone with you."

"Let her do it." Fannie knew George's grudging words were more concern for his own investment than for Toni's well-being, but she was grateful just the same.

Both women were untied, and Toni slumped to the ground, limp as a rag.

Tears nearly blinded Fannie as she studied her friend's injuries. Purple-black bruises covered her, and her face was swollen nearly twice its size. Her nose was twisted and bloody, clearly broken. Swallowing hard, she noted the sunken cheek. At this moment, she hated George. He had smashed Toni's face in. Even if there were a doctor nearby, the shattered bones would never heal properly. If she pulled through, Toni would never be the beauty she had been hours before.

Fannie shook herself from the thoughts. Beauty wasn't the immediate concern. Life and death. Those things were all that mattered for now. Once again, she found herself calling upon God's mercy. For the first time in her life, she was utterly hopeless. *I can't save her alone, God.*

Turning to the men, she spoke around a choking lump. "Give me something to wipe the blood off."

None of the men moved. "I have to have something to clean off the blood."

"Here." Willard handed her a clean handkerchief and a canteen of water. "I wouldn't have hurt her."

"Shut up, Willard, you measly coward," George sneered.

"I wouldn't have." He directed his words to Fannie. "Why do you think I didn't take you? I would have had to hurt you or Mrs. Barnes that night, and I wasn't willing to do that."

"If you're looking to apologize, it's a little late, Willard."

His eyes clouded over. Desperation. In a beat, his pistol came out of his holster and he stepped back, pointing his gun from George to Tom to Clay. "Don't move." He turned to Fannie. "Get their guns."

Head spinning by the turn of events, Fannie was too stunned to disobey. One by one, she divested the men of their weapons.

"Now. I have a proposition for you two," Willard said to Tom and George.

Fannie swallowed her disappointment and went back to

tending to her friend while the men negotiated which dismal future she and Toni and the twins would face.

She wiped the damp cloth over Toni's face, cleaning the dried blood from her nose and mouth. She put the canteen to Toni's lips and let the liquid dribble in. Toni gave a soft moan. Tears welled in Fannie's eyes again, and she nearly fainted with relief.

"Let's go." Willard grabbed her arm and hauled her to her feet.

"What do you think you're doing?"

"It appears these two men aren't in the mood to negotiate, so you are coming with me. I'm sure Blake Tanner will pay a pretty penny to get you back."

"Willard!" a voice echoed off the hills. Fannie's heart raced as she recognized the source.

"Willard," Blake called again. "Drop the gun."

"I'll shoot her!" Willard's voice had taken on a high-pitched tone of panic. "I mean it."

"I don't think so. You want to see your wife and children again, don't you?"

"My wife doesn't want me, thanks to you."

The three men standing defenseless in the middle of camp snickered. Willard swung around. "Shut up!"

A gunshot cracked through the air, and Willard's pistol flew from his hand as he let out a startled yell. He lunged for the weapon. Blake strode into camp on one side, Sam on the other, and another scout whose name Fannie did not know. "You four are surrounded. Do you really want to go for that gun, Willard?"

He didn't even have to consider the question. Willard backed away and lifted his hands up high.

"You'll have to shoot us," George said valiantly. "I'm not going to stop trying to get her back until I get all my money."

"Same here," echoed Tom, with more bravado than bravery, as evidenced by the tremor in his tone.

"I have a proposition for you," Blake said.

Tom scrutinized him. "I'm listenin'."

"In my saddlebag I have twice the amount that Fannie and Toni gave me to keep for Katie and Kip."

Fannie sucked in a breath. "What are you doing?"

Blake ignored her, keeping his pistol and gaze fixed on Tom. "I'll split it between the two of you." At their stupid expressions, Blake expounded. "You'll each come away with twice what you started out with."

"What about me?" Willard whined. "What do I get out of this little bargain?"

Blake swung on the sniveling coward. "You get to ride away and never show your face again."

Willard hung his head, knowing he had no more cards to play.

"What about my pay?" Clay broke in.

"That's between you and the men who hired you."

Tom and George exchanged glances. "What if we say no?" George asked. "I could make a lot more money keeping Toni working for another couple of years."

"If she lives." Sam's hardened tone sent a slither of fear through Fannie. He gave her his pistol. "Keep this on those men." He knelt beside Toni and tenderly lifted her into his arms. His gentleness took Fannie's breath away. He cradled her in his arms and took her to the wagon.

Fannie forced her attention back to Blake and his bargaining. "If you don't take the offer, I'll find a real lawman and turn all four of you in for kidnapping and theft. So you have a choice. You can either walk away with twice as much as you had before, or you can get turned in to the sheriff in Blythe Creek. I'm sure he'd be interested to know how you passed around a fake Wanted poster in his town."

Fake? Fannie drew a breath as her mind wrapped around this news. If that was true, then she was safe. She and the twins would truly be free of Tom forever.

"Fine. We'll accept."

"Good." Blake turned to Fannie. "Untie the twins and use those ropes to tie these men together."

"What are you talkin' about?" George said, his voice filled with suspicion.

"Here's what's going to happen." Fannie marveled at the calmness of Blake's voice. "You are going to be tied up. I'm going to put the money bag between you. You should be able to get loose eventually. And when you do, I expect you to go back to your lives and figure out how to live without Toni, Fannie, and the twins. Because I'll never be this lenient again."

Within minutes, the men were tied up. As they prepared to leave, Fannie gripped Blake's hand. "Thank you for coming after us."

"I'm sorry I let you go in the first place." He gave her a

look of intense promise. "I'll never let you go again."

Her mouth dropped open at his declaration.

"Let's go. I want to get as much distance between these characters and us as we can, or I might change my mind and just shoot every one of them."

Blake assisted her into the wagon. Fannie poked through the back. "How is she, Sam?"

Sam's voice was grave. "She's in and out of consciousness. She will need a lot of time to recover. I pray she'll be all right."

"The sooner we get her back to camp, the sooner we can have Sadie take care of her like she took care of Fannie," Blake said.

Fannie lay in the dark listening as, one by one, the camp settled into sleep. So far Blake hadn't come to claim the debt she owed him. Minute after minute passed, and then one hour and two, and still he hadn't come to her. Why? Blake wasn't mercenary. He wasn't trying to frighten her. She sat up with a gasp as realization dawned. He must be waiting for her. She cringed at the thought of how angry he must be after waiting for so long. Her insides began to quake. What would Tom have done if she had ever made him wait like this? Granted, she knew in her heart that Blake wasn't like Tom, but he was a man, wasn't he? He'd paid money for her, hadn't he? Fannie hoped he didn't think her ungrateful for making him wait.

She knew she should get up. She tried to will her legs to move but couldn't. Not yet. She wasn't altogether sure her legs would hold her. She hugged her knees to her chest and watched Blake where he lay, alone across the campsite. The twins slept soundly next to her. Toni still lay unconscious in the wagon where Sam watched over her. Grant Kelley stood vigil somewhere close by. Blake was expecting her. A tear slipped down Fannie's cheek. Once more, she had only one source of payment. And again, she had no choice but to pay.

Blake awoke to movement next to him and sat up with a start. Fannie sat next to his bedroll. "What are you doing?" he demanded.

"You bought me," she said simply. "I figure we should get it over with." Slowly, she lay back.

Get it over with? What was she—?

His breath caught in his throat as understanding rifled through him. She thought he expected—? He scrambled away from her. "Honey, I don't want this from you."

Relief and confusion wrestled across her features in the light of the low campfire.

"I don't understand. Then why did you pay the money?"

"So Tom would leave you alone. I would have done it for anyone."

Her expression fell. "I see. Well, thank you." Rising, she turned her steps back to the wagon.

Blake watched Fannie walk away, her shoulders drooping. He could only imagine the shame she must have felt. As much as he wanted to assure her how desperately he wanted her, he'd never accept her as compensation for something he'd gladly paid. Better to let it go for now.

He settled back on his blanket, staring into a cloudless sky.

A lump settled in his throat as he thought of how close he'd come to losing Fannie forever. Thank God he'd been saving for his land all these years so that he'd had the means available to pay her ransom. He wished he could make her understand that he'd given the money gladly, expecting nothing from her, but hoping his act would show her how much he cared.

He closed his eyes and began to drift off amid images of a cross, nail-scarred hands, and tender smile, and finally, he understood what Sam had been trying to tell him all these years.

The sky began to lighten, and Fannie hadn't slept a wink. The camp hadn't stirred, except for once, when Grant Kelley switched with Blake, who still stood watch. When she could no longer bear to lay still pretending to sleep, Fannie roused and walked to the wagon to check on Toni. Sam's head rested in his hands as he sat cross-legged on the wagon bed next to her.

Fannie climbed into the wagon and sat on her knees, watching her friend's shallow breathing. "Any change, Sam?"

He looked up, his eyes weary, face lined with worry. He shook his head. "Not yet."

Determination hardened around his mouth. This man wasn't about to give up hope. Fannie was stumped. What sort of men were these? They weren't real. They couldn't be. Surely some day, Blake would come around collecting.

"Why'd he do it?" she asked.

Sam frowned, his eyes filled with question. "Why'd who do what?"

"Blake. He gave everything he's been saving. Now he can't buy his land."

An understanding smile tipped Sam's lips. "I reckon he figured you were more important than land. There's plenty of land to go around. It'll still be there when he saves again. There's only one of you."

"He said he'd have done it for anyone."

Sam shrugged. "Maybe, maybe not. But he didn't do it for just anyone, did he? He did it for you."

"I can't pay him back," she whispered, tears forming. "I hate being beholden to anyone."

"Did Blake indicate you owe him anything?"

"No. He won't take . . ." Heat burned her cheeks. "Never mind."

Sam covered her hand with his. "Miss Caldwell. I'd pay every cent to see Toni open her eyes. And when she did, my joy would be full just knowing she was safe. I wouldn't ask her for payment"—he gave her a pointed look—"of any kind."

Fannie's heart ached with longing to understand. She'd been paying for so long, the thought of not owing anything was almost beyond her grasp.

She stared at Sam, willing him to help her trust Blake's motives.

"He says he doesn't want anything from me."

"Then you'll have to believe your safety is enough for him."

A shout of victory rose from the pioneers when they reached camp the next evening. Weary and heartsick, Fannie found it difficult to match their enthusiasm. Especially when Mrs. Kane tearfully returned the twins' things. "I guess I truly wasn't meant to be a mother."

How did one respond to something like that? Thankfully, Fannie was spared the necessity because Mrs. Kane didn't stay for a response.

That night the stars seemed brighter, the moon bigger, and the sky a velvet blanket filled with promise for a future and a hope. Fannie wasn't quite brave enough to sit outside the circle against the wagon wheel as she had once done. But she craved solitude, so she perched on the tongue and allowed the beauty of the night to surround her with peace.

Footsteps interrupted her solitude, and she looked up to find Blake standing next to her. Her cheeks grew warm as she remembered her conduct last night. She knew she owed him an apology. "I-uh—"

Before she could get the words out, Blake thrust her money forward. "You'll be needing this now."

"Don't be ridiculous. That's only half of my half. It may take me a while to pay you back the rest. But I will. I promise."

"You don't owe me anything, Fannie."

"Yes I do. And if you won't take payment in other ways," she said pointedly, "you must accept the money."

Blake stepped forward. He set the money down on the wagon seat and took her hand in his. "Fannie, listen to me." He pulled her to her feet. "When I said I would have done it for anyone, that wasn't true. I paid the money because I care about you, and I wanted you safe."

Fannie stared wide-eyed and tried to grasp what he was saying. "You care?"

"More than care." Blake stared down at her, his eyes so earnest, so warm that Fannie felt the urge to snuggle close to him, press her cheek against his chest, and stay there forever. He slipped both arms around her and pulled her close. "I love you. And if you love me too, I want you to marry me. Then I'll take you into my bed, but not because you owe me, but because we're man and wife and we've vowed before God to love and cherish one another."

His words sounded so beautiful, Fannie couldn't keep back tears. "But what about the money you spent, Blake? Sadie told me you had saved and saved so you could stop being a wagon master."

He nodded. "I'll have to do one more wagon train. But as my wife, you can file a claim and live in Oregon with the twins."

Fannie's heart nearly leapt from her chest, and she couldn't look at him as she tried to find the courage to say yes. "Okay, then."

"What?"

She looked up and stared him in the eye. "I said okay then."

"Okay, what?"

"What do you mean? You just asked me to marry you."

A slow smile touched his lips, and Fannie was enchanted to be the recipient of such a beautiful sight. "I said, if you love me too, I want you to marry me."

Frustration welled inside of her. "Well, I know that. I have ears."

"Oh, Fannie. Is everything going to be a fight between us?"

"I don't know what you want from me, Blake."

"All I want is your love. We can work out the rest. But I have to hear you say you love me."

All of Fannie's resolve melted, and she took a step closer and wrapped her arms around his neck. "I love you, Blake. And if you want me, I'll marry you."

He grinned and lowered his head.

Fannie spoke up. "But . . ."

A frown creased his brow, and he moved his head back. "But?"

"The twins. They go where I go."

He chuckled and pressed a kiss, warm and tender to her forehead. "I wouldn't have it any other way."

Fannie felt a heavy weight fall away from her, and joy that she hadn't known since before her pa's death lifted her to her tiptoes. "Just remember," she said with a lilt to her voice. "You're going into this with your eyes wide open."

"Stop talking, Fannie."

She did, and his lips covered hers as he enveloped her in an embrace that promised forever.

Dear Reader,

Beginnings are always so exciting. Beginning a new series, a new book, being one of the launch authors for a new line of books like Avon Inspire. But sometimes following through is a challenge. The new wears off pretty fast. And then the struggle begins. Especially for someone like me with a short attention span.

Even through the struggle of trying to finish this book, *Defiant Heart* never got old to me as I wrote from day to day. And at the time that I write this letter, it's been several days since I turned in the book to my editor, and I'm still thinking about Fannie, Blake, Toni, Sam, and the twins, anxious to begin the second book in the Westward Hearts series so I can see how they're all doing. I feel like I knew Fannie and desperately wanted her to find happiness—with God and with the man of her dreams. I wanted to create a heroine who had a lot to overcome, but found grace in the end. Fannie learned that redemption means someone else pays and you owe nothing. There's an old song we used to sing:

He paid a debt He did not owe
I owed a debt I could not pay
I needed someone to wash my sins away
And now I sing a brand new song "Amazing Grace"
Christ Jesus paid a debt that I could never pay.

Powerful. Powerful. Powerful. In Blake, I wanted to create a man who had a lot to lose and was willing to lose it to save the woman he loved. He was the character who personified the sacrifice Jesus made for humanity. Just like it is difficult to grasp sometimes that Jesus doesn't expect us to work off that payment,

Fannie had trouble at first realizing that Blake was willing to pay for her and let her go, if that's what she wanted. But how much better for her that she agreed to become his bride?

I pray that as you read *Defiant Heart*, Jesus shows you how wild He is for you.

All things new. . . .

Tracey Bateman

Discussion Questions

1. Blake has a problem trusting women because of his mother's past. How does your upbringing affect your current relationships for the good or bad?

2. Do you think Fannie (and Toni) had the right to take the money when they left Hawkins? Why or why not? What would you have done in their situation?

3. Why do you think Sam is able to look past Toni's sins and into her heart?

4. Do you know someone with a tarnished past and wish you could give them the benefit of the doubt? Are you the one who is trying to change but find it difficult to convince people around you of your sincerity?

5. Throughout Fannie's early childhood she had a happy family life with two loving parents. Suddenly her world was upended when her father died. What could her

mother have done to spare her children their hard life after her death?

6. Why do you think no one came to Fannie and the twins' rescue from Tom? After three years, surely someone noticed they were being abused. How far have we come as a society where child protection is concerned?

7. What steps do you think Fannie should take to learn to forgive those who have hurt her, including the stepfather who sold her to Tom in the first place? How does her inability to forgive keep her from moving forward in her life?

8. Both Fannie and Toni are willing to risk everything to have a chance to start fresh out West. Has there ever been a time in your life when you were considering taking a huge risk for a new opportunity?

9. Throughout *Defiant Heart,* Fannie is incredibly brave, headstrong, and stubborn. Her very strong points can sometimes become weaknesses. When does that happen? Do you have any attributes that can become burdens?

10. When Fannie realizes that Blake wants nothing in return for paying her debt, she is able to make the parallel to Jesus. Discuss this debt-cancellation as it pertains to mankind.

Turn the page for an exciting preview of

DISTANT HEART

The next book in the Westward Hearts series
by Tracey Bateman
Coming Soon from Avon Inspire

The wagon dipped and swayed in the deep ruts of the well-worn trail, making it awfully difficult for Toni Rodden to sew a straight line. Some might call her crazy for even trying. For that matter she hadn't missed Eliza Shelton's smirk as the woman sashayed by with Lucille Adams just moments ago, but Toni was beyond caring what those catty women thought. Her mission was clear: get Fannie's wedding gown finished before the silly girl gave in (and Toni had no doubt she would) and married Blake Tanner long before they reached Oregon. Toni was determined. Fannie might not have the church wedding she dreamed of, but at the very least, she'd have a new dress.

A sting pinched her neck and Toni let out a yelp.

On the wagon seat next to her, Fannie Caldwell gripped the reins in a white-knuckle hold, fighting the lumbering team of oxen as they struggled to keep their footing in the deep ruts. She eyed Toni, only for a split second, before yanking her gaze back to the weightier task. "What happened?"

she asked, breathlessly, bracing her feet against the plank floor, her body barely in the seat as she showed the enormous animals just who was boss.

"Dadburn horseflies!"

Toni swatted at her neck, but it was too late to do anything about the would-be assassin that flew, bit, and buzzed away like the tiny harassing bullies they were. Bad enough to be layered in dust every single day for the last three months, nearly swept away by gusty prairie winds, but the horseflies . . . they were the worst. Still, she had no real reason to complain, considering the alternative: working in the rooms above George's saloon. She preferred the wind and caked-on dust—even the horseflies.

Toni knew she'd had a close call with that last beating. George had truly almost killed her. But never again. He was out of her life forever. Blake and Sam had seen to that. And after all these years of entertaining men so that George could line his pockets, she had finally won. Yes. She, Toni Rodden, had finally won for the first time in her twenty-two years. George thought he'd ruined her by smashing away her beauty. How wrong he'd been! Freedom rose within her like a victory flag and she wanted to shout to every man who didn't give her a second look, "That's right. Turn away, don't look at me, I don't want you to. Maybe now you'll leave me alone." The crooked nose and caved cheek, which dropped her left eye lower than her right, had marked the end of life as she'd known it. The end of her beauty. The glorious beginning of a new day.

She mopped at her sweat-soaked neck and wished like

the dickens an errant cloud would cover the sun, if only for five minutes. A little relief from the torturous heat. Even a soaking cloud burst would be welcome. On such miserable days, it was difficult for the travelers to remember that August would soon give way to autumn, then things would cool down. For now, tempers were as short as the days were long and it didn't take much to set anyone off. Feuds were springing up left and right, the most notable among them, between Zach Kane and Kurt Adams—all because of a dead chicken. Lucille, Kurt's wife, swore up and down that Zach's half-wolf pup had killed the fowl and Kurt had no reason to disbelieve his little wife. The two had come close to a duel until Blake put a stop to the foolishness. The travelers, in desperate need of a distraction had begun to take sides. A dead chicken and a naughty pup had split a three-hundred-member wagon train down the middle. Toni had to shake her head at the nonsense. Although secretly she figured, *Pups will be pups, keep the chickens in a pen.*

And anyway, for the last two days, an unspoken truce remained in effect. Folks had other things on their minds. Fort Laramie, for instance. The wonderful distraction lay just ahead. And beyond that, the mountains, and beyond that . . . the promised land. Oregon.

Once Toni had dreamed of that land of milk and honey as her new beginning. A husband. Children. All the things a woman held in her heart from childhood. But with one look at her unattractive new face, she'd forever buried those romantic notions. Now her dreams hinged on two things: her skills as a seamstress and the short memories of her fellow travelers. Since she was no longer a threat, she hoped the women of the train would extend mercy and not sweep aside their skirts forever when they saw her coming.

Eventually, she dreamed of owning a little dress shop. Until then, she could mend tears and make shirts for men who were without wives or mothers to sew for them. But none of that would happen if she couldn't make a fresh start in folks' minds.

If what Sam Two Feathers said was true, all of her past sins were behind her. All things were new in God's eyes. And they truly were for Toni. In more ways than one. In Fort Laramie, she would test her theory and her new face on the soldiers.

Fighting against the heat and dust, she sat next to Fannie, her dearest friend and traveling companion, and worked the deep green cotton of Fannie's wedding gown—fabric donated by Sadie Barnes, a widow and friend.

"I wish it were silk," she mourned to her friend. "A woman should get married in white silk and lace."

Fannie smiled. "Cotton is more serviceable and white would be a disaster. I need something I can wear on other days."

"I suppose you're right." Toni gave a sigh. And truly, the green gown would be beautiful against Fannie's mass of red curls, but a young bride should wear a silk gown of white—and after all the pain Fannie had endured, she especially deserved to be wrapped in a vision of loveliness. "Brides have no business being so practical," she grumped.

Fannie flicked the reins, spurring on the oxen. She laughed at Toni's comment. "Practical. I'm sure you'd never convince

Blake of such a thing. As a matter of fact, he thinks I'm rather impractical to be sewing a new dress in the first place. He thinks we should get married as soon as we find a preacher and not wait until we get to Oregon. But I don't want to start our life together as a married couple on the trail. Marriage is hard enough without making it harder. But it's becoming more difficult to convince Blake to wait until Oregon. He—um—thinks there's a preacher at the fort."

A rueful smile tipped Toni's lips. "Well, he is a man after all."

Fannie's cheeks darkened. "I know, but . . ."

Toni finally understood. After three years of abuse at the hands of a man who had treated her like a slave, Fannie was afraid of the intimacies of marriage. Toni reached out and touched Fannie's forearm. "Don't worry. Blake might be a man, but he's a man in love. He'll wait for you."

"Is it fair to him?"

"Honey, this is about what you're ready for. Be honest with him. He'll understand. At least I'm sure he . . ."

Toni's voice trailed off and she turned her attention back to her sewing. What did she really know about men in love anyway? Men who lusted, she knew all about. Men who were obsessed, men who used women's bodies but had no interest in capturing a heart, those men she had enough firsthand knowledge of to fill volumes of books, but she had no experience with men who loved the way Blake so clearly did.

As a matter of fact, Blake's devotion to Fannie had turned every woman's head in the wagon train, including Toni's, but she knew better than to dream of love for herself. In particular, now that her looks were gone, she would never have the opportunity to discover what it felt like to be loved. But then, she never really had that option before either. Better to be ignored by men than wanted for all the wrong reasons.

Sam Two Feathers watched over Toni with the patience of Job. Waiting . . . but not sure what he was waiting for. He knew he was a fool to dream of her the way he did, but easier to rip out his own heart than to stop its wild beating every time she came near. And she had no inkling. None. He was sure of it. She honestly believed her loss of physical beauty had somehow made her less desirable. If only she had any idea of her true worth. Four weeks had gone by since her terrible ordeal at the hands of the man who owned the saloon where Toni had once been a prostitute. Four weeks since Sam had sat by her bedside, praying night and day for God to bring her back to him. After only three days, she was fully lucid. Five days later, she was back on the wagon sitting beside her friend and traveling companion, Fannie Caldwell, and within two weeks, her bruises were almost gone. Now she still bore the physical evidence of her brutal beating, but her eyes twinkled more, her voice lifted with merry peals of laughter, and her forehead was void of worry lines for the first time since he'd met her.

She looked up as he drew near on horseback. "Hi, Sam." Her smile captivated him, as it always did. Combined with white-blonde hair, that smile was the most amazing thing he'd ever seen and each time she turned it on him, he was utterly done in.

"We'll be circling outside the fort in about an hour," he said as soon as he found his voice. "Captain Roland has given us permission to camp for a few days and trade at the trading post inside the fort."

"Oh, good. I hope they have some ribbon," Toni said. "If Fannie can't have silk, the least I can do is weave some ribbon into the neckline."

Sam felt his lips quirk into what he knew was a stupid grin. He couldn't help it. Toni was completely unaware that her true beauty lay deep inside and revealed itself in loyalty, wit, intelligence, and honesty. Those characteristics were more attractive than all of her other beauty combined: beautiful silky hair, eyes as green as the lush Oregon valleys, lips that invited a man to test their soft fullness. He'd spent too much time thinking about those things. But even more time wondering how to break through the thick chains she kept wound around her heart. He knew there could never be anything between them, but if nothing else, he desperately wanted her to discover that she was worth loving.

"Was there anything else, Sam?" Fannie asked, her voice tipped with amusement.

Heat rushed to Sam's neck and for once he was grateful for the beating sun. He shook his head, swallowing hard and searching his mind for words.

Toni turned her smile on him once more. "Thanks for letting us know about the fort, Sam."

He gave her a nod and tipped his hat, then rode down the line to the next wagon, the image of her sweet smile burned into his mind like a hot brand. Sam knew he had no right to fall in love with a woman like Toni. His mixed blood—half Sioux, half white—combined with his decision to live in the white man's world, condemned him to loneliness. Society would not allow him to marry a white woman. It wasn't possible. But he couldn't quite convince his heart to stop throbbing in his chest at the very sight of Toni. A smile from her lips weakened his knees and the sound of her laughter held him captive.

Thirty minutes later, he positioned his horse next to wagon master and best friend, Blake Tanner. "Everyone ready?" Blake asked.

"I think so."

"The Blaines' pup tied up?"

Sam gave a solemn nod. "Yeah, but he's not happy about it. Neither is Zach. Mrs. Kane's worried the dog's going to hang himself pulling against his rope so bad."

"Too bad. That animal's a menace. We should have left him where we found him."

Sam said nothing. He agreed with Blake in one sense, but they both knew that ever since Mrs. Kane lost her young daughter in a twister a couple of months ago, she'd mourned terribly. Finding the half-wolf puppy shivering and abandoned on the plains had filled a void in her heart and started a process of healing the jagged tear left by the death of her only child. "I'll keep an eye on the ornery pup."

"See that you do, or I'll have Zach take him out and shoot him." The tension in Blake's voice raised Sam's concern. It wasn't like him to be this insistent over something so petty.

"Somethin' wrong, Blake?"

The wagon master kept his gaze on the fort ahead as the wagon train inched closer and closer to the wooden gate. His jaw clenched, his eyes squinting against the glare of the noon-day sun. "Fine."

Whatever it was, his friend needed coaxing to share. And Sam didn't coax. He figured a man had a right to his own thoughts, and unless he chose to open up, it was no one else's business what was going on in his head.

Blake expelled a heavy sigh. "I wish we could go around the fort."

"We can." Mildly surprised, Sam looked at him askance. "You're in charge."

Pursing his lips, Blake appeared to consider the thought for a minute. He shook his head. "No. Folks haven't had a break from the trail in too many weeks. And two of Captain Randall's hunters came back with antelope. They've been roasting them. The scouts have told us the women at the fort are preparing for a real feast."

Again, Sam kept silent. And Blake continued. "Maybe a diversion'll stop the petty arguments we've been having to put up with lately. That Kane puppy is just one issue lately. There's the squalling Adams' baby that keeps everyone within ten wagons either way awake half the night, the heat is getting to everyone, and the thought of climbing the mountains soon has the whole company nervous."

Sam nodded. "I was thinking of holding a prayer service before we move on from Fort Laramie. You have a problem with that idea?"

Blake gave his hat a two-fingered shove and swiped the

sweat from his brow with the back of his arm. "Might not be a bad idea. We'll need all the extra help from above that we can get." A barking flash of black and gray fur tore out past them. Blake let up a growl as he fought to keep Dusty, his stallion, from tossing him to the ground. "Especially if Kane doesn't do something about that ornery dog."

Tracey Bateman

Photo courtesy of the author

TRACEY BATEMAN lives in Missouri with her husband and four children. Their rural home provides a wonderful atmosphere for a writer's imagination to grow and produce characters, plots, and settings. In 1994, with three children to raise, she and her husband agreed that she should go to college and earn a degree. In a freshman English class, her love for writing was rekindled, and she wrote a short story that she later turned into a book. Her college career was cut short with the news of their fourth baby's impending arrival, but the seeds of hope for a writing career had already taken root. Over the next several years she wrote, exchanged ideas with critique partners, studied the craft of writing, and eventually all the hard work paid off. She currently has over twenty-five books published in a variety of genres. Tracey believes completely that God has big plans for his Kids and that all things are possible to anyone who will put their hope and trust in God.